# BIKER BOYS

# BIKER BOYS
## GAY EROTIC STORIES

EDITED BY
CHRISTOPHER PIERCE

Published in the United States by Cleis Press Inc., 2246 Sixth St., Berkeley, California 94710.

Printed in the United States.
Cover design: Scott Idleman
Cover photograph: John Burke/Superstock
Text design: Frank Wiedemann
Cleis logo art: Juana Alicia
First Edition.
10 9 8 7 6 5 4 3 2 1

ISBN: 978-1-57344-396-8

# Contents

# I INTRODUCTION

When I was given the opportunity to edit an erotic anthology about men and motorcycles, I decided my mission would be to bring together the hottest, most diverse biker stories I could possibly find. I believe I was successful.

The *Biker Boys* party gets started in style with Simon Sheppard's classic "Two Bikers in a Room at the Motel 6." Sheppard perfectly captures the doubt, excitement and danger that occur whenever two men of the road size each other up and are forced to decide if it's worth the risk to hook up or not.

"Taken," by Wayne Mansfield, and "Chrome-Obsessed," by Pepper Espinoza, perfectly describe fantasies shared by millions of gay men, this editor included. Xan West's "Ready" is an extraordinary tale of catharsis and redemption that hits you equally in the heart and between the legs.

"Tulsa," by Dusty Taylor, tells the tale of a hard-edged love triangle between three bikers, each with secrets that cannot be concealed much longer if any of the men are to survive.

Always brilliant Jeff Mann closes the volume with another of his masterpieces, "As It Flies," which, like all of his work, is an intelligent, wistful and unbearably hot story about two men longing for and loving each other.

Now straddle your hog and get ready to burn some rubber: enjoy the stories.

Christopher Pierce
Boynton Beach, Florida

# TWO BIKERS IN A ROOM AT THE MOTEL 6

Simon Sheppard

Harleys are all about pussy. Big-time pussy." Duane smiled.

Trev didn't know quite what to say to that, so he remained cautiously silent and kind of smiled back.

Duane reached over for a pack of American Spirits.

"Mind if I smoke?" he asked, not waiting for an answer before lighting up. He leaned back in the chair, legs spread, and blew smoke rings. Trev tried to figure out just what was happening. He looked again at Duane, sitting there just feet away wearing nothing but a black T-shirt, white off-brand briefs, and thick gray socks. The T-shirt had a picture of a flaming skull. Trev gave up trying. But he knew damn well how he'd ended up there, in a cheap motel room at three A.M. with a man who was going on about pussy.

He'd been heading for home, still had an hour or two to go, twisty mountain roads having given way to freeways with an endless procession of Dennys, Jacks, and Wendys, when he'd pulled into a nonchain coffee shop for a jolt of caffeine. He'd been walking through the parking lot, helmet in hand, when he spotted Duane standing by his Harley Softail Fat Boy, the bike all chrome, fringed saddlebags, and just-waxed gleam. They stared at each other the way two men who probably aren't gay but might be do. After one long moment, Duane nodded.

"Hey, bud," he said.

Trev figured *What the hell* and walked over. The man had a pug-handsome face, a longish ponytail, and when he smiled Trev could see he was missing an incisor. It was one of those stupid movie moments. There were cars all around them in the spotlit parking lot, hungry people coming, well-fed people going, but all Trev could see was Duane standing there, midthirties, maybe even forty, in jeans and leathers, smiling. It wasn't because the man was particularly good-looking. It wasn't because he was Trev's type—he wasn't that, either. He might even have very well been straight. It was just one of those stupid things that happen sometimes, those times when your dick should know better but gets hard anyway.

"Can I buy you a cup of coffee?" Trev asked, hoping such a noncommittal invite would give nothing away.

"I got a room next door," the man said, gesturing toward the neighboring Motel 6, mute testimony to affordable lodging. "And I got me a fresh fifth of Jack Daniels in the room."

"I shouldn't drink. I'll be riding home."

"Just one." The man smiled that missing-tooth smile again. If this wasn't a flirtation, it was a passable imitation. "I'm Duane."

"I should make sure my bike's locked up." Trev walked over to his motorcycle, Duane in tow. Trev took the U-shaped Kryptonite lock from its mount, locked it through a spoke of the front wheel. He was acutely aware that Real Men used chains.

"Nice bike," Duane said. Trev stared hard, looking for a

hint of condescension. The motorcycle in question, a Suzuki Bandit 1200, was sleek and powerful; from a standing start, it could most likely have left Duane's chromed-up Harley in the dust. But it was a sport bike, not a cruiser, and worst of all it was Japanese—a "rice-burner," the object of hard-core Harley riders' contempt.

"Thanks."

"Looks like it would be real fast." Not a trace of irony in his voice. Trev wondered if irony entered into Duane's life at all. "Real fast."

When the two of them got to the room, Duane hung out the Do Not Disturb sign, winked when he locked the door, then pulled off his big boots, unbuckled his ornate H-D belt buckle, and let his jeans fall to the floor like it was the most natural thing in the world to strip down to underwear in front of a man that he'd just met. Duane's legs were squat, muscular and very white.

"All about pussy," he repeated one more time, as though neither of them had heard it before. "Must be why you ride a Suzuki."

"Um…" Trev said.

"Got me all the pussy I can handle. Course, I was married. Still am, really, till the divorce becomes final. But it just didn't work out. For one thing, she didn't like how much I was on the road. See, I repair and customize bikes for a living, and I spend a lot of time out scouting for old Harleys to fix up. That's where I just came from. Found a '66 Sportster that I wanted to check out before I bought it and had it shipped back home. So, Trev, what do you do?"

"For a living?"

"Yeah."

"I teach."

"Kids are great." Duane smiled that missing-incisor smile of his.

"I teach college."

"You look kinda young to be a professor." Duane stubbed out the American Spirit and spread his legs wider. Trev couldn't help but steal a glance. Briefs well-filled, by the look of it.

"I'm a teaching assistant."

"What do you teach?"

*Here it comes,* Trev thought. "British literature, mostly." He probably should have said something butch, like economics.

Duane reached down and scratched his balls. The unself-conscious maleness of the gesture made Trev's cock throb.

"Yeah," Duane said, "she was jealous of me, which was screwed up because I let her fuck around all she wanted, which was with other girls, mostly."

"Double standard, eh?" Trev made his voice sound as sympathetic as possible.

"You know it, man." Duane tugged at his ponytail, then pulled off the rubber band. His hair fell to his shoulders, an unlikely halo. "Guys are only as faithful as we have to be, right?"

"You got it," Trev said, wanting to strike just the right tone of conspiratorial cocksmanship. He thought back to Barry, beautiful Barry with the perfect nipples and improbably big cock. They'd been together almost a year, back when they were both in grad school. But Barry had wanted their relationship to be open, Trev had resisted, and finally Barry left him, at first tomcatting around the bars, then settling down with the prof who'd taught them Woolf and Strachey. Presumably the teacher's focus on Bloomsbury had made him less monogamously inclined.

"...get fucked up the ass." Trev's attention had drifted away, but that sure snapped him back.

"Huh?" he said stupidly. "The ass, you liked fucking her up the ass?"

"You sure you're paying attention?" Duane grinned and slid his right hand under his T-shirt. "No, man, I'm the one who likes to be fucked up the ass."

"Oh," Trev said stupidly. "Maybe I will have that drink."

"Help yourself." Duane gestured to the bottle. Trev got up to fetch a glass from the bathroom, rearranging his crotch en route.

"I discovered when I was a kid," Duane continued, "that I liked playing with my asshole, liked the feeling. Becky and I tried one of them strap-ons, but it didn't do the job. A man's cock, that's what does the job." He pulled off his T-shirt. His torso was white and nearly hairless, with clear lines of demarcation where his arms and neck had gotten sun. There were two tattoos, one on each pec. On the left was a bird, a bluebird or something, done fairly crudely. On the right was a swastika.

Trev didn't want to know.

"Only thing is," Duane continued, taking a swig of Jack straight from the bottle, "too many fags want to kiss and shit. And most of 'em want to take it up the ass. I don't do that, fuck guys—I ain't a queer. All I want is to get fucked. But I'm sure you'd like it either way, huh, Trev?" He reached over and touched Trev—who was not sure about the tack this was taking—briefly on the knee.

Trev kind of froze. A weak "So you think I'm gay?" was all he could manage.

"Dude, I'd bet the fucking farm on it. Why do you think you're here?"

Trev exhaled.

Duane leaned back, hands behind his head, his bushy armpits

in stark contrast to his otherwise smooth flesh. "So how about it, professor?"

"You want me to fuck you? Just like that?"

"You're dick's hard, ain't it?" Duane rose to his feet, hands still behind his head, and walked over to Trev, who was sitting uneasily on the edge of the slightly saggy bed. The biker shoved Trev's legs apart with one knee, sliding his left leg between the seated man's thighs. Close up, Duane smelled like tobacco and white trash.

"Hey, uh..."

"Fuck man, just fucking relax." Duane took a little step closer, pressing in until his leg was against Trev's swollen crotch. "Yeah, you're hard, all right," he said. "So how about it?"

Trev looked around the room, at the TV on the dresser, the mass-produced prints on the wall, the Gideon Bible next to a little pile of condoms in the half-open drawer of the bedside table. Anywhere but at the well-filled pair of white cotton Y-fronts that hovered inches from his face.

"How fucking about it, Suzuki-boy?" Duane pulled the front of his briefs down and a big hard dick flopped out, pubes even bushier than armpits, cock even whiter than the rest of him, foreskin still half-hiding the swollen head.

Trev wanted to, he wanted to take that dick between his lips, down his throat, suck it dry. But he didn't. Some things were just more than he bargained for, and at times like that he got reticent, he got shy.

"Shy, huh?" Duane backed off and let his underwear fall to his feet. Wearing only socks, like in some cheesy porn video, he turned his back and slowly, deliberately walked back to the chair. His back was covered with tattoos, all the way down to his narrow waist. "Your fucking loss."

*Yeah*, Trev thought, *my fucking loss*. The biker's ass was beefy, muscular, and absolutely perfect. Without thinking, he reached out and touched it, touched the man's right asscheek.

Duane looked back, hair swinging around his shoulders. "That's it, professor. You want it, huh?"

Well, yeah, Trev did. He wanted that biker ass, that butt that was usually perched on a Harley but that could be his for the night. All he had to do was say yes.

"Yes." Just like that.

"Well, you'd better get your fucking clothes off, then." Duane raised the bottle and poured more whiskey down his throat. "If you're gonna fuck me." Unspoken was: *If you're man enough.*

Duane put down the whiskey, bent over and spread his cheeks. His asshole had a surprisingly dark corona and a distinct pucker. Well trained. Well used, apparently. Trev reached down and gave his hard-on a squeeze.

"What're you waiting for, Suzuki-boy?" A taunt, a challenge, an invitation.

Trev stuck his thumb in his mouth, getting it wet with spit, and then pressed it up against the biker's hole. Duane's ass was hungry and very hot, nearly sucking in his thumb. He slid it farther in, the slick tunnel opening right up for him.

"How you want it?" Trev asked, taking back his finger.

"Hot and heavy."

"I mean, you like being on your back?"

"All fours. That way you can't look in my eyes and get all romantic."

"Then get on the bed." Trev hoped the sneer in his voice didn't sound too forced.

The biker did as he was told, posing doggy-style, his ass offered for use. Trev pulled off his boots, jeans and boxers. He left his socks and T-shirt on; he figured if he was going to be in cheesy porn, he might as well look the part.

"Okay, fag," Duane rumbled, "let's see how good you can fill me up." That was it—no more preamble, no foreplay, just Trev's dick inside a stranger's ass. And he could live with that.

Trev reached into the bedside table for a condom. Fishing around for lube, his hand met something cold and hard and metallic.

"Hey, professor. You gonna fuck my ass or what?"

Trev, startled, pulled his hand from the drawer. "Just looking for some lube."

"Over there."

Trev had to admit it: there was something about the whole situation that made him uneasy, though nothing disturbing enough to deflate his erection. Maybe his cock thrived on danger, be it riding his 1200 at eighty miles an hour down a freeway crowded with cell phone-talking SUV drivers, or riding the ass of a debatably straight redneck with USA's THE BEST, FUCK THE REST tattooed on his right shoulder blade. He unrolled the rubber over his thickish cock. He'd make it through this. He'd perform.

Duane reached over to the bottle of whiskey and took another swig. "Ah, that's better," he said. "Now let's get that prick of yours up my ass."

Trev squirted a big glob of lube in his hand and rubbed it down the crack of the biker's butt.

"Man, that feels great."

Trev's first two fingers found the man's hole and slid inside.

"Fuck, yeah. Yeah."

The inside of the biker was smooth and welcoming. Trev knelt behind him on the bed and positioned his cockhead up against the guy's asshole.

"Just shove it right in," Duane said, his voice suddenly soft around the edges. "I can take it. I've took bigger things than that." He looked back over his shoulder and smiled his missing-tooth smile. "No offense."

"None taken," Trev said, and he rammed his dick home.

"Unh."

Trev had to admit it—Duane's hole felt great. Actually, Trev hadn't fucked anyone in months, and his cock was happy to be plugging an eager ass again. He put his hands on Duane's smooth, pale hips and started thrusting.

"Faster, dude."

Trev speeded up his stroke.

"I said faster, faggot." Trev felt a sudden flush of dignity—*Nobody's going to treat* me *that way*—but instead of pulling out and leaving, he grabbed a handful of Duane's hair and slammed in hard.

Trev gritted out, "You take it, you fuck." Where had *that* come from? Virginia Woolf would have been appalled.

But Duane wasn't appalled, he was excited, and he started thrusting his ass backward, impaling himself on the younger man's hard shaft.

"That's it, dude. Screw my fuckin' ass."

Trev wasn't sure just how he felt about being bossed around by a man with a swastika tattoo  it was just as well Duane didn't know that his last name was Cohen. But Trev did know how being up the biker's ass felt. It felt absolutely great. All the way in, he reached around Duane's smooth thigh and grabbed at the man's cock. Trev was pleased to note that it was hard as steel; he himself could never stay hard while he was getting fucked. Maybe he was just not enough of a bottom. Or maybe, unlike Duane, he just wasn't enough of a man.

"Let go of my dick," Duane said. "I'm not ready to come yet."

But Trev was ready for the whole thing to come to a climax.

He'd been riding all day, and his tired thighs were starting to tremble. He looked around the motel room, at the leather jackets lying in a corner, at the half-empty bottle of whiskey, and suddenly all he wanted was to be back on the road, gliding through the freedom of curves. He speeded up, bringing himself to the edge of orgasm.

"Oh, man, that feels so fucking great that feels so fucking great," Duane moaned. But Trev didn't care anymore, if in fact he ever had. With one final push, he made himself shoot a load into the rubber, a jet so strong it was almost painful. He caught his breath and slid his dick out of Duane's ass, a load of milky cum filling the rubber's sagging tip.

Duane was silent for a moment, then said, "I gotta get off. Suck my dick."

"Listen, I'm not your wife."

"Fair enough," Duane said. He flipped himself onto his back and started beating off, long foreskin sliding back and forth. He reached his other hand around to his ass and started playing with his slippery hole. And within moments it was over, cum oozing out of his piss-slit, pouring onto his belly.

Trev was already on his feet, looking for his pants.

"Hey, what's the rush?" Duane slid his hand along his belly, then brought it to his mouth, slurping off his own jizm.

"Gotta get going is all. Have a long ride ahead of me."

"Stay for a shower and another drink." It sounded less like an invitation than a command.

"No, really, thanks but…" Trev could smell the guy's asshole on his cock.

"Oh, man…" Duane's voice sounded suddenly softer, less like a hard-bitten biker's than a disappointed child's. Trev looked into his eyes, and something—probably whatever drew him to Duane in the first place—led him to agree to stay.

When he got out of the shower and wrapped a towel around his waist, he found Duane still lying there naked, the cum almost dry.

"Pour yourself a drink and lie down," Duane said. Trev filled the glass with whiskey and lay back down on the bed. He hesitated for a moment, then began to stroke Duane's leg. The tracery of a scar ran most of the way down his thigh, even paler than the rest of his skin.

"Pins and rods. I've gone down so often that my body is held together with pins and rods."

Trev winced and took a slug of Jack Daniels. His towel fell open, revealing his just-washed dick.

"Man," said Duane, "you're a really good fuck. Thanks. Thanks a lot."

"No problem," Trev said, which seemed like a fairly stupid thing to say.

They lay around talking and drinking, telling each other things they might not have said to anyone they actually knew. If this all had been a semi-romantic cliché, they would have discovered that they weren't so different after all. But the more Trev learned about Duane, the wider the gaps between them seemed. It was, after all, only sex, just dick into ass, that had brought them together.

Somewhere toward the bottom of the bottle, Trev slurred, "You know, I think I'm in absolutely no shape to get on my bike." But Duane was already on his way to passing out, eyes shut, breath slowing. Trev wobbled into the bathroom, took a piss, and made sure the motel room door was double locked, in case some maid got overenthusiastic. He crawled into bed beside the unconscious biker, drew his fingertips over the still-unexplained swastika tattoo, and fell fast asleep.

Around seven, Trev woke with a *Where the fuck am I?* start.

Sunlight crept through the imperfectly shut drapes as, careful
not to wake Duane, he gathered up his clothes and got dressed.
He was about to leave when he remembered the object in the
bedside table. He carefully pulled out the drawer. There it was,
what he knew it would be: a gun, a biker's shiny handgun, just
inches from the Gideon Bible. Involuntarily, he drew in his
breath.

"You like it?" Duane had woken up.

"It's just...I'm not used to guns."

"Don't worry about it. So you're heading out?"

"Miles to go before I sleep." Trev wasn't sure that Duane
would even get the reference.

"Sit over here for a sec," Duane said. Trev lowered himself
to the bed and Duane propped himself up and awkwardly gave
him a hug. And then, astonishingly, the biker kissed Trev on the
lips, softly but decisively.

Trev didn't know what to say, so he said nothing, just slowly
stood up and walked toward the door.

"Keep the rubber side down and the shiny side up," Duane
called after him, already lighting up a cigarette.

"Yeah. You too," Trev replied, closing the motel room's door
behind him. In a few hours, he'd be hundreds of miles away.

# ENGINES OF
# THE NIGHT

Landon Dixon

Mariano stepped out from a shadowed corner of the night-deserted city, into the halo of light shed by a lone streetlamp.

Far off, the high-pitched whine of an engine throttling to top speed wailed through the night, with another chasing after it. Then came the shotgun-like blasts of a bigger engine, exploding from cruising to racing speed, echoing through the dark, empty, concrete streets.

The sounds of the engines tearing the night apart filled Mariano's ears. He nervously glanced around, saw nothing, so stepped out of the light and walked down the blackened sidewalk, hips swaying, bum shivering, swishing from side to side. He was dark haired and doe eyed, young, with velvety olive skin and full red lips, dressed in a tight white T-shirt and tight pair of faded blue jeans. Like most of the city's population, he'd never been out at night.

He was halfway down the block when a light suddenly blazed

out of an alley farther up the street, something coming to life. An engine revved lean and mean close at hand, and the white light flashed off the abandoned storefront windows and swept out into the street, capturing Mariano in its fiercely glaring beam.

"Oh, Jesus!" the young man gasped, staring into the light, frozen.

The engine screamed. And a rising cloud of white smoke palled out from the back, the acrid smell of burning rubber filling the air, the light bearing down on Mariano. He cried out and dashed for the alley on the other side of the street, the engine wailing like a banshee in pursuit.

He wasn't going to make it: the street was too wide, the machine too fast. He stumbled and fell, and the engine revved triumphantly, almost right on top of him. And then...*boom!* Another engine came thundering to life, blasting out of the black mouth of the alley and slamming into the other speeding engine.

The Harley broadsided the Yamaha, thick rubber front tire pushing up, heavy metal chopper forks driving forward, smashing into the lighter bike and sending it sailing through a store window, glass exploding into the night.

The Harley screeched to a stop at the curb, throbbing with power, chrome headlight spotlighting the shattered window. Mariano watched from the pavement on his hands and knees, his pretty face sheened with sweat, eyes shining and body panting.

The Yamaha let out an angry shriek and righted itself. Rubber squealed on tile, and the bike mounted the shattered window and bounced out onto the sidewalk. The two riderless motorcycles faced each other, engines roaring, tailpipes fuming, frames twisting and tires burning. Mariano screamed and jumped to his feet and ran blindly off down the street.

The Yamaha instantly veered left and flew past the Harley,

catching the young man in its headlight again, zooming onto his heels. The Harley backed up with an angry growl and blasted off in pursuit. Mariano cut right into an empty lot, the Yamaha twisting, skidding, jittering past down the street on smoking tires, then straightening out and chasing back, leaping the curb and tearing into the narrow lot, its full-throttled cry reverberating off the brick walls on either side.

Mariano flung his head around, arms and legs pumping wildly, and was blinded by the burning orb of the Yamaha, closing fast. His feet touched the asphalt of a back lane, and he spotted another light, off to his left—the Harley—heard the tremendous rumble of its huge engine as it roared up.

Mariano flew down the lane, the two motorcycles in pursuit. The Yamaha was faster, quicker, more agile than the Harley, and a flat-out rundown on open road was just its meat. But first it had to make the turn before it could rocket, and full speed eluded it.

Because the Harley had already been thundering down the straightaway at one-hundred-per, too big and too strong at top speed to let anything get in its way, its front tire slammed into the Yamaha's rear tire and the Yamaha shuddered, wobbled, lost speed.

The Harley hit it again, turning the bike sideways on the asphalt. Then it rammed into the skittering machine and pitchforked it, lifting and carrying the motorcycle screaming on its chopper up the lane and past Mariano, the young man gaping at the sight of the big bike bullying the other forward at a fearsome speed.

The Harley blew out into the street, headed straight for the brick wall of a warehouse, cradling the vainly revving Yamaha in its chopper. Then it slammed on its brakes, and its tires dug into the pavement, the Yamaha flying off its front end and thirty feet into the solid brick wall, smashing against the blank, unyielding stone with a sickening crash.

The Harley jackknifed to a stop in the middle of the street as the Yamaha shattered against the wall, coming to pieces in a hail of shrapnel. The machine crashed down onto its side, smoke and steam billowing from its wrecked metal frame, one wheel spinning. The Harley bellowed a deep-barreled roar of triumph and spun around in a smoky blue circle, then bore down on Mariano.

The motorcycle easily and expertly scooped the stunned young man up on its customized chopper and roared down the street, rampaging right out of the city and deeper into the pitch-black night, tailpipes blazing.

"Good boy!" Sledge said, when the Harley deposited Mariano at his feet. He patted the throbbing machine on the headlight and tenderly ran his scarred hands over the scratches on its chopper forks, before feeding it oil and gas.

Then the huge, balding man with the sissy-bar nose stud and handlebar goatee dragged Mariano to his feet and looked the young man over. He grinned with brown, broken teeth, his bloodshot eyes traveling all over Mariano's slim, lithe body.

"I—I was just out for a walk," Mariano gasped, staring at the hulking biker. "I was...curious."

Sledge honked out a laugh.

"Curiosity killed the pussy," he growled.

He thrust out an oil-pan hand and clutched the back of Mariano's slender neck, roughly jerked the man's head forward, and slammed his thick, cracked lips into Mariano's dainty mouth. The Harley revved, shining its spotlight on the two men.

Mariano struggled against Sledge. But the big biker held him tight and close, grinding his mouth against Mariano's, chewing on the plush, red lips, sucking up the tangy-sweet scent of the guy through his billowing nostrils. Then he grasped Mariano's T-shirt at the shoulders and tore it down and off, flung it aside. His dirty hands smacked up against the young man's smooth, tight chest, greasy fingers digging into taut pecs.

Sledge's gripping, groping hands almost lifted Mariano right off his feet, the biker's exhaust steaming into his open mouth. Then the man thrust his cinderblock head down and lashed one of Mariano's burnt-sugar nipples with his gearshift-pierced tongue, then the other tender, hairless bud. Mariano whimpered and squirmed, and Sledge sealed his lips around a pert nipple and roughly sucked. Then he bit, just about tearing the pebble-ringed jutter right off Mariano's heaving bronze chest.

"I ain't here to service you, bike bitch!" the big man suddenly rasped. He hitched his bent-fingered hands into Mariano's jeans, yanked them down. The young man's pants puddled at his sneakers, his cock springing up long and hard and golden in the light of the rumbling motorcycle. Sledge licked his lips, staring at Mariano's smooth, bobbing penis. Then he tore off his leather vest, grabbed Mariano by the back of the neck and yanked him into his grizzled, muscle-cleaved chest.

Mariano deftly cupped the big man's heavy pecs in his soft, slender hands, his slim fingers sliding through the thick mat of salt-and-pepper hair and taking hold. He stuck out his long, neon-pink tongue and threaded it through the brush, the searching tip touching up against a rigid, fiery-red nipple. Sledge grunted and jerked, and the bike jumped.

Mariano swirled his tongue all around the groaning man's bud, painting it with his hot saliva, teasing it harder and thicker, then doing the same to the other straining nipple. He squeezed Sledge's hairy, muscle-ribbed pecs, head bouncing, tongue dancing between the man's nipples. Then, lips puckering, he began kissing and sucking.

"Fuck!" Sledge roared, in a voice as deep-barreled as his bike.

He slammed Mariano down to his knees, crotch level. "You want something to suck, here's something to suck!" He jerked the zipper on his cruddy jeans down and dug around for his cock, found it and thrust the stubby appendage into Mariano's shining face.

The young man gripped the biker's road-wide hips and stared at the thick, vein-piped cock twitching out of a wild bush of black pubes. He breathed on it, making it jump, his wet, brown eyes gleaming. Then he laced the hot, throbbing shaft with his fingers and took the bloated cap into his mouth.

"Fuckin' cunt! Suck my cock!" Sledge howled, sinking his crude fingers into Mariano's glossy brown hair, the Harley digging up dirt with its rear wheel.

Mariano pulled on the man's mushroomed hood, lips sealed tight, sucking hard and fast, feeling the heated pulse of the biker in his mouth and his hand, the thunder of the bike through the ground. He loosened his grip on the shaft and pushed his head forward, sensuously sliding his lips down Sledge's cock, consuming the man.

Sledge bucked and groaned, heavy hands riding Mariano's moving head as the kneeling young man's nose parted his pubes, lips kissing up against his tight, wrinkled balls. Mariano slithered out his tongue and licked Sledge's nut sac, mouth full of the man's cock. He brought his head back, then forward, sucking wet and hard on Sledge's pulsating prick.

"Tailpipe time!" the big biker finally gritted, pulling Mariano up by the hair and shoving him against the side of a shack he sometimes called home. He kicked the guy's legs apart, smacked brazen, bronze butt-flesh with the flat of his hand.

"Oooh!" Mariano cried, shivering.

The smell of oil grew even stronger. Sledge smeared his cock, then Mariano's crack. His thick, rough fingers slid along the silken crevice and poked at the puckered hole, making Mariano gasp and quiver.

Sledge rocked the young man's tight little bum with another fat *whack*. Then he gripped his greased cock and plunged it in between Mariano's buttocks, hitting the guy's starfish and driving through until his huge thighs slammed up against Mariano's trembling cheeks, cock buried in ass, the motorcycle surging forward like a dog on a chain.

Sledge grabbed hold of Mariano's shoulders and geared up his hips, pistoning hot, tight bung with his cock.

"This is what you wanted all along, huh, bitch?" he rasped, ramming Mariano's asshole. "This is why you were out on the fuckin' streets at night!"

Mariano bit his lip and moaned, violently rocking in rhythm to Sledge's savage cock-thrusts, the biker's pipe scorching his chute, the Harley throttling up and down with every wicked stroke. Sledge torqued up the pressure still more, pumping the young man's gripping anus in a frenzy. His chewed-up nails bit into Mariano's shoulder blades, Mariano's bum and body and the decrepit shack shrunk with the big man's furious pounding.

"Yoowwrr!" the biker and the bike roared, blowing Mariano's ass apart. Sledge's thundering cock exploded, blasting white-hot semen up into Mariano's bowels.

Mariano suddenly spun around, flinging his legs up and twisting his body in a quick, agile move that took Sledge completely by surprise. He crashed the tire iron he'd gathered up off the ground down onto Sledge's head. The shocked biker staggered backward, blood pouring out of the trench in his skull, cock still spurting, sprinkling the dead yellow grass.

Sledge crashed down to his knees, too stunned and slow to

react, the panting Harley bathing the grisly night scene in fiery light. Mariano clubbed Sledge again, and the man toppled face-forward onto the hard ground and lay still. Mariano dropped the bloody tire iron, pulled up his pants and ran over to the Harley, mounted it.

"This is why I was out on the street tonight," he breathed, stroking the idling machine's curved, gleaming gas tank, covetously clutching the shiny chrome handlebars. "And now I'll get the men *I* want."

The powerful engine rumbled between the young man's tingling thighs; the big bike was ready for action.

# ZIGGY

## T. Hitman

I set the keys down on the counter next to a week's worth of mail and newspapers. The sound of the television in the living room and the fact that my neighbor's dog hadn't greeted me at the door with his usual bark told me their son had finally shown, as expected. I cut through the kitchen into the living room. The Carsons' lab woke with a friendly growl from where he lay beside the couch, wagged his tail and lumbered over to me. I patted the old dog's nape and noticed the back of a man's head propped up on one arm of the couch, the lump of the body under a blanket. Two big feet in white socks hung over the couch's other end, and a deep, manly snore filled the room.

I let the dog out, ushered him quietly back through the kitchen door once he'd finished his business, and was about to head over to my house on the far side of the Carsons' flawless lawn when the sound of footsteps reached my ears. I turned to see the youngest of the family's three sons, Ziggy, plod sleepily into the room. I suddenly forgot all about my plans for a lazy November

Sunday as I stood facing the intense blue gaze of the black sheep of the Carson clan, the one his dad called *the biker*.

"Mornin'," I said, giving a nervous wave. "I'm Archie."

"Yeah, I figured," the man with the hard, good looks said, extending his large bear paw of a hand. I accepted the gesture and secretly melted as his strong fingers squeezed down on mine. As we shook, I remembered what I'd been told about him—thirty-three years old, recently divorced, the troubled son. I found myself unintentionally sizing him up, drinking in the image of his raw and masculine presence from the brush-cut top of his head down to those big feet in their white boot socks.

I pegged him at being a few inches taller than me, six two, six three in height, his body tight and muscled in all the right places. He even looked like a Harley guy in his black T-shirt and old blue jeans. But nothing was more telling of his love of motorcycles than the day's worth of stubble on his hard, square jaw, which ended on his chin in a long, wispy goatee.

"So, you're the biker guy," I said.

Ziggy broke our handshake and scratched at the meaty full-ness of his package, adjusting it.

"Yup. And you're the new neighbor, the queer guy," he growled.

My eyes snapped up off his crotch.

"*Huh*—?" I sputtered.

Ziggy opened the fridge and pulled out the OJ. As stunned as his last comment left me, his rugged handsomeness overwhelmed me more. I focused on his hairy throat when he chugged down a gulp right out of the carton, shocked by how sexual the act looked.

"The folks said you were watching the place and walking the dog while they're in Vegas," he said between swallows.

"And they told you I was...gay?"

Ziggy nodded and belted out a loud burp. He leaned against the counter, his tired blue eyes narrowing on me. As I stood there, he toyed with the lump between his legs.

"You want to see the hog?" he asked.

I tried to answer, only to gag on the hot coals in my mouth. Truth was, I would have given my left nut to see Ziggy's "hog," but not the souped-up beauty of his Harley with its powerful engine, polished chrome and leather seat.

"I'd love to, but I got some shit to do," I said instead, horrified that I'd begun getting stiff from the mere sight of him. I cut out quick, walked across the Carsons' lawn, crunched through about a foot of leaves covering mine and headed into the house to jerk off over "the biker."

That afternoon, less than a full quarter into the football game, I heard the crunch of footsteps and looked out to see Ziggy climbing the steps to the deck outside my living room. A jolt of excitement rushed through my insides as he knocked on the sliding glass door. I jumped up and opened it.

"Hey, Ziggy—what's up?"

The biker shuffled nervously in place, big hiking boots now on his feet. "You got any beer?"

I did, so I said, "Sure, come on in." Ziggy plodded into the house. "It's only the light stuff, though, sorry."

"That's cool," he said. Over my shoulder, I saw him eyeing the television. "You like football?"

I returned from the kitchen with two cold ones and handed Ziggy a can.

"I love football."

"Must be all those sweaty guys in their tight uniforms," he growled in a menacing voice. I was starting to realize it was his tough-guy's brand of humor, not an insult.

"That, too," I chuckled before taking a swig. When I lowered my beer, I found Ziggy still staring, one cold blue eye narrowed on me.

"*What?*" I asked.

He opened his can and knocked back a sip.

"You're not what I expected when they said there was a gay dude living next door."

Coolly, I asked, "And what did you expect?"

Ziggy shrugged. "I don't know, somebody with lots of cats who likes arranging flowers, I guess. Not a guy who drinks beer and watches football."

I plunked down on the couch in front of the tube.

"Sorry to disappoint you."

Ziggy hovered in place a few seconds longer. I sensed in his silence an edge of anticipation, as if he wanted to ask me something but just didn't know how. Finally, he joined me at a respectable distance on the opposite end of the couch.

"I just meant that you seem like one of the guys."

"That's probably because I am."

Ziggy leaned back on the couch. I felt his stare upon me in the silent, tense seconds that followed.

"Then that must mean you got some porn kicking around here," he eventually said.

The cold beer in my stomach instantly soured.

"Sure, some," I admitted. In fact, the DVD I'd whacked off to earlier that day was still in the player.

Ziggy's handsome, hard face broke into an unexpected sexy grin.

"I figured you did. Dude, I ain't seen anything more exciting than the same old pussy rag I brought with me when I got here, and I've trashed that," he said. I didn't catch on to where he was leading, due mostly to the fact that the thought of him stroking his cock made mine ache. "The folks don't got a computer or anything but basic cable, so I've been shit out of luck trying to find some excitement around here. Hell," he sighed. "I'm hurting so bad, I'd even watch two dudes screwing at this point."

His statement caught me completely off guard.

"Yeah, right," I said, shifting on the couch in an attempt to make my throbbing hard-on appear less obvious. But I quickly learned Ziggy wasn't joking.

"Put something in," he said. "Show me how homos suck each other off."

I reluctantly reached for the remote and hit the PLAY button. The movie picked up right where it had made me shoot a few hours before, the football game replaced by the throaty moans of some gym stud getting his bone slurped on by a young blond twink.

Ziggy sat back up, a stunned look on his handsome face.

"*Fuck!*" he grumbled in disbelief. "I ain't had my carrot hummed on like that since before I was married, and even then, she didn't do half as good a job as I bet one of you guys would."

I tipped my attention from the TV to Ziggy to see that he was really getting into it. His eyes were glued to the intense cocksucking taking place on the screen, and I noticed, to my surprise, he'd put down his beer and had both hands on his lap, covering what looked to be an even more prominent bulge.

"Well, we *homos* love to give head," I said. My heart now drummed in my ears as the truth of where all this was going began to set in. "So of course, we do a better job than women."

Ziggy's eyes suddenly met mine, and I knew what it was he'd really come to my door in search of.

"You a good cocksucker?" he posed, his deep, manly voice no longer holding a threatening rumble but something of a desperate plea.

Boldly, I reached over and slid my hand onto his outer thigh. The biker didn't protest.

"I give awesome head, dude."

Ziggy reclined on the couch, exposing what I already knew to be true: his dick was just as hard as mine.

"Then do it, guy," he croaked, throwing one arm behind his head. His free hand gripped the back of my head and coaxed me down. "Suck my fuckin' cock and make me feel like a king!"

He didn't have to ask me twice. Licking my lips, I lunged for his zipper. I quickly had Ziggy's jeans open, exposing the well-packed fullness of the tighty-whities he wore beneath.

"Sweet," I muttered, huffing a hot breath across the tent in his shorts. I eased the cotton flap aside and reached into the hairy warmth, freeing two bloated, spunk-filled bullnuts and what had to be seven straining inches of the meanest looking cock I'd ever seen. Coarse chestnut-colored shag ran up Ziggy's column. A fat fireman's helmet capped his pole, fresh precum glistening from its pisshole. I dipped my tongue into the gummy liquid and savored its taste.

After swabbing Ziggy clean, I buried my face in his musky-smelling balls and licked the sweaty skin of his nuts. Before long, he was leaking more precum and begging me to suck him off.

"Come on," he growled. "*Gag on me, you fucker!*"

Wasting no time, I sucked the head of Ziggy's cock between my lips. He seized up beneath me on the couch, moaning his approval at the incredible feel of my mouth on his knob. Figuring that he hadn't been blown since before his divorce, I made sure to give him the best I had. Opening fully, I gulped him all the way down to the root, then spit most of his cock out until just the head was perched on my tongue. I alternated between deep-throating him and sucking only on his cockhead, the whole time toying with his fat, hairy nuts. The taste of Ziggy's precum grew gamier the longer I worked his shamefully neglected dick, and soon, I'd teased him right to the edge.

*"I'm gonna cream, you hot fucker!"* he growled into my ears as he fought to hold back from spraying. I eased up, then plunged down one more time. On the next upward stroke, Ziggy flooded my face, pissing six shots of jizz into my mouth. I held his spunk on my tongue as his orgasm petered out, then swallowed him down, something not lost on him. "Dude, you even *drank* it," he sighed.

I looked up to see a wide grin on his handsome, sweat-streaked face. Licking my lips, I moved to stand, but Ziggy's hand on the back of my neck prevented me from leaving.

"Put it back in your mouth," he growled. I did as he ordered, to find his cock hadn't even begun to get soft.

I gave Ziggy head two more times before the end of the football game, and later that afternoon, he took me for a spin on his other hog.

# BIKER DUDE

## Shane Allison

I was parked at a dead end of the lake.

Coming out really gets the adrenaline flowing. The anticipation of getting my dick sucked, or the pleasure of having one in my mouth gets the loins stirring. I love the thought of a couple of hikers stumbling upon me blowing some filthy, tobacco-chewing redneck in some bushes. The lake is where I come when I want to be whorish and slutty, getting fucked by...who knows?

But the day I was out, there weren't too many around—not even families barbecuing and swimming. There were a few older dudes trolling about, but all they did was play cat-and-mouse around the lake. I had been out since noon. I'd woken up that morning with a hard-on from hell, and all I could think about was dick, men filling every fucking orifice of my body. I couldn't even eat breakfast due to having cock on the brain. I usually jack off to soothe the morning wood that sprouts up in my underwear, but I wanted more than that. I wanted a pair of country lips around this thing. I needed a tongue to lick these balls and drain them dry. Men love my dick. *Not too big and not too small* they tell me. I just wished I knew where they were keeping themselves on this Sunday afternoon. Maybe they were doing the church thing with the family. We Southern folks love to go to church.

When I get like I do, I don't care if you're ugly, fat or fem; as long as you can suck a dick, you're cool as shit in my book. I was going to be pissed if I left after being out all day and hadn't gotten sucked or fucked.

It was so quiet. There wasn't so much as a bird chirping, just the rustle of leaves blowing across the road.

Out at the lake you never know who's going to ride up on you. I remember when it used to be hot with guys. You could come out any time of the day or night and get off. I used to sneak out of my folks' house at three in the morning and make the forty-five minute drive down Sam Allen Road to see who was prowling about through the trails. And there was always one or two walking ass-naked down the dirt roads. Those were the ones I liked best 'cause they were into anything.

When the sheriffs got wind of men having sex in the woods, they started busting us and blocked off some of the pathways. But you think that stopped us? We just designated another area. They wouldn't have this problem if Tallahassee had a bathhouse, a safe place we could go without having to worry about getting busted. North Florida is so fucking conservative.

After I'd been waiting half the day for dick, suddenly a guy on a motorcycle was hauling ass up toward me. He looked familiar. Yeah, I had seen him out before. Everybody has tried to get at him, but all he does is circle around the lake on his motorcycle. I love the hell out of some biker dudes, though. This one was a wet dream in motion, black leather jacket with a confederate flag embroidered on the back with denim and leather chaps to match. My dick was thumping crazy just thinking about his calloused mitts groping my butt, his thick mustache pricking my sensitive skin, and, I hoped, that dick infiltrating my preppy ass. But I've never seen him get with a black dude, just station wagon–driving granddaddies. I walked up on him getting sucked off on Lutterloh Trail one time when I was out there. Biker didn't bat an eyelash when he saw me crouched down in some bushes beating off to the blow job work some daddy was giving him against an oak tree. As a matter of fact, he started moaning and going on, putting on a show just for me.

I couldn't have been happier to see him. I had a lot of jizz swirling around, and he was just the motorhead I needed to release some tension. It was just my luck that he circled around and parked his bike directly behind me. My car window was down. I had my dick out. My meat had a mind of its own that day. A teardrop of precum had settled at my piss-slit. I rubbed the clear, sticky juice along the bulbous head of my dick. I watched the motorhead's moves from my rearview mirror as he got off his bike. The chaps accentuated the bulge in his crotch nicely. He pulled at it as he walked toward me. Beads of sweat poured down my face. My ticker was like a time bomb in my chest. My gut felt like there were tiny spiders crawling around inside it. The click of his biker boots grew closer as I massaged my dick. Precum steadily oozed forth.

I dig men like him, rough around the edges. He was just my type: bad to the bone. He placed those calloused hands of his inside my driver's-side window. I nestled deep into my seat, so he could get a good look at the naughty thing I was doing.

"How you doing?" he asked roughly.

"What's up?" I said.

I beat my dick against the steering wheel.

"How long have you been out?" he asked, as he took my

dick into his big, meaty hand. I adore another man's hand on my dick. He felt hot and I was rock-hard in his palm. I tensed in the car seat as he jacked me off. I could see myself in his shades making those orgasm faces I do. He smiled at me, knowing I was pleased with his touch.

"I'm a little nervous up here on this road. You want to go somewhere that's private, so we won't be disturbed?" he asked, steadily jacking me off.

I could hardly get a response together the way he was working my pud.

"Yeah, let's go," I said.

I tucked my hardness back into my jeans and zipped up. The biker waited as I got out, rolled up the windows and locked my car. We walked side by side into the woods. We kept our talk small as we made our way along a narrow trail, deeper into the forest.

"How long have you been out here?" he asked again with a redneck twang.

"Since about two thirty," I replied.

"Has there been anyone out here?"

"Just a few here and there circling about, but no one that I really wanted to get with until you came along."

The biker laughed, stuffing his hands down into the pockets of worn chaps that he looked so good in. He sported a nice bubble butt I hoped to hold on to if it was ever going to get to the point of my ass being fucked. I tailed behind him until we got to a clearing where a foam mattress was conveniently lying. Beer cans and empty potato chip bags were strewn about like someone had been there.

"Is this yours?" I asked.

"Yeah, I like to come out here sometimes at night and just drink under the stars. It's nice."

"You're not scared of something crawling up on you and biting you?"

"Critters are just as afraid of us as we are of them," he said. "Besides, I got *this*."

He pulled out the biggest fucking knife I had ever seen. The kind you see in pawnshops locked behind plate glass for a reason. I stopped and stood staring at him as he brandished a blade that was big enough to bring a fucking pachyderm down.

"Relax, I just carry it around out here." His explanation put me at ease. "This thing is actually outlawed in this part of Florida. I could get arrested if I'm caught with it," he said.

"So, no one's going to see us out here?" I asked.

"Not this time of day on a Sunday, no."

The two of us sat down on the dirty foam mattress had the faint whiff of pee, but I kept my mouth shut about the smell. He kicked off his boots and I untied my shoes. He pulled off his vest and folded it over a branch. I was hesitant to take off my clothes. I had gained back all the weight I'd lost and then some after moving back home from New York, but I said fuck it. It wasn't like I was marrying the motorhead. I tossed my shirt to a nearby branch, but it landed in the dirt.

The biker undid the copper clasp of his chaps and jeans and peeled them off his legs, which had a moderate amount of fur. Suddenly, I didn't feel so inadequate about my love handles. He had no idea about my hair fetish. I developed it in high school after fucking this guy named Jeff whose hair was thicker than normal. Kids used to pick on him in P.E. 'cause he was so hairy. A fucking teenage werewolf, this guy was. The girls were freaked out, but shit, he wasn't into pussy anyway. We used to mess around three times a week after school. He'd come over to my house and we would suck each other off. He wasn't into getting fucked. He felt like less of a man if he took it up the ass—but enough about him.

The biker's dick was nothing like I imagined, but quite larger with bolts of veins running along the shaft. It curled up like a coat hook and a barbell ran through the piss-slit.

"What is that?" I asked.

"It's called a Prince Albert," he said.

"Shit, did that hurt?"

"No, not really."

I took down my jeans and pulled them off my ankles. We were both naked as jaybirds and were up shit creek if a park ranger stumbled upon us. Being from such a small town, I have to be careful who sees me. I can't knock over a garbage can without running into someone who knows me or knows my cousins, third cousins and so on.

Gnats were hovering in my ears, and mosquitoes were buzzing about, out for blood. It was what I hated about the lake, about being outside period, but the only thing that was about to get the best of my ass was this biker, and if he wanted me as badly as I wanted him, it was about to be on and popping.

"Do you kiss?" he asked.

Normally, I wasn't into it, but since I liked bikers, I made an exception in his case.

"Yeah," I said.

He started to get rough with me right off, taking me behind my neck and pulling me forcefully to his bearded mouth. He reeked of dirt and stale beer like he hadn't showered in days. His facial hair felt course against my supple, sensitive skin. He kissed me harder than I had ever been kissed, sucking my tongue into his mouth. His 'stache felt scratchy. I took him by the back of his neck and pressed him closely into me, pretending I was into french kissing. I kept my eyes open as his were closed. In his arms, I felt like a young virgin about to lose his cherry to a drunken wino.

"Suck my nipples," he said, pushing my head to his chest, which was overgrown with peppered fuzz. I tongued his pink, perky nip as I gawked at his dick peripherally. He toyed with it as I worked his big nipples. I reached in and felt for his dick, massaging it a bit. From his groaning, it seemed like he approved of what I was doing.

"Get on your knees," he demanded.

I felt him move in behind me. The biker pressed my back into the foam that smelled of pee. His fingers tickled as he parted the cheeks of my dark-skinned ass, and then I felt something cold and wet teasing my hole. He was eating me out. His tongue up my butt drove me bananas. After sitting in a hot car for five hours, I was sure my butt was good and ripe. He pulled the glutes of my booty farther apart in his need to get in deeper. I clawed at leaves and earth as he rimmed me. I could feel drool trickling down my scrotal sac. He took my dick and pulled at it like a cow's udder. That feeling sealed the deal.

"Eat me," I said. "Eat my black fucking butt, guy."

He moaned to my dirty talk.

"Jesus, fuck!" I yelled. We were deep in the forest, so the only things that could see and hear us were the animals.

Motorhead spanked my butt, then pulled my hips hard to him.

"Get that ass up here," he said.

I could feel his Prince Albert traipse along my ass.

I heard him hawking spit in his palm. He slathered my hole with his ready- made lubricant. I couldn't have been more excited about what was about to go down: I was about to feel what had to be eight thick inches of biker dick being maneuvered up my insides. I thought of my dildo at home and how I used it to stretch my rectal muscles every night for six months. Dicks that were too large to fuck me before started to fit like a glove.

"I'm going to fuck you until you die," he laughed.

"Fuck me, leather daddy. My ass is all yours."

I felt him pushing the head of his dick in easily.

"Ah, fuck, daddy," I said. "Get it in me, man. Get that dick in me, fuck!"

It hurt in the beginning, but once all his meat was packed snug in my booty, it was heavenly.

"You got a hot ass, boy," he huffed, bucking wildly on the turf of Mother Nature. I waved mosquitoes and gnats out of my face as he used my behind. I felt his pace slowing until he pulled steadily out of me. He groped my hips and pushed me over onto my back. He hawked another glob of spit into his hand and slathered me and his rod with the stuff. The biker tugged me to his dick like I was some burly sack of sand and eased his sloppy, filthy meat back up my hot sphincter. He threw my legs over his hairy shoulders. I held on to the edges of the foam mattress as he rode my slutty ass.

"This black butt is yours, daddy," I said.

"Is it? This ass is mine?"

"Yeah, yeah, daddy, yeah," I said.

The biker gave me a mean fuck that Sunday afternoon. I could have gone on for hours. I looked at the squirrels above me jumping from branch to branch as he worked my butt. When I looked past him, I was startled when I saw someone standing in the bushes. Tree trunks and Spanish moss hid his face, so I couldn't make it out. I saw a flash of white that could have only been the voyeur's underwear through his open fly. I thought if he was a cop, we would be on our way to lockup by now, but he just stood there, rubbing his crotch to my being fucked.

I liked that we were being watched but was a little afraid he would attract other onlookers.

"I think we got company," I told the biker. With his dick

buried deep in my butt, he turned to see who we were being watched by. The biker waved him over and continued plowing my ass.

Sweat was burning my eyes and the bugs were merciless. The voyeur stood over me blocking the sun's cruelty. It was Kevin, another biker I've had at the arcades at the local adult video store. I'd sucked his dick a few times. Kevin was heavyset with long, gray hair done up in a ponytail with a bristling beard to match. His big belly hung over his belt, but he had a dick for days, and wasted no time forking that well-hung piece of meat and set of low-hanging balls out of his open jeans. He kneeled down over me and fed me his dick.

Kevin fucked my face as the biker took it out on my ass. Kevin's pubes tickled my nose as he worked my mouth. The stink of dirt and biker musk was everywhere.

"Take my fucking cock, man," said Kevin. I stared into his bloodshot-blues as he churned my mouth. I held on to his hips, pulling his dick deep into me. Kevin's face was flushed and blushing when he uncorked his dick from my mouth and shot thick streams of cum on my chest and belly. He wiped what was left on his jeans, tucked his dick back into the safety of his underwear, and left me and the biker to our own devices. I was sure to see him again fucking the face of some popper-drunk, dick-craving twink back at the 'cades.

"I'm close," whispered the biker. Drops of his sweat fell in my face. He pulled out of me and straddled my burly body. He held his dick over my mug and waved it back and forth like a pendulum.

"Open your mouth," he demanded. When I did what I'd been told, he packed it full of sweaty biker dick. Within seconds, he shot forth a flood of semen and I swallowed every creamy drop. I lay there on the mattress with cum drying on my chest and wallowing around in my gut while he dressed himself, pulling chaps and jeans over his bare, hairy butt.

"You comin' out tomorrow?" he asked.

"If you want me to, yeah," I told him.

"Good. I'll look for you around this time."

"Me and my ass will be ready," I said, as I stuck my finger up my fucked asshole. I watched his butt as he walked out of the woods, underbrush breaking under his scuffed black shit-kickers.

# WILD CHILD

## Christopher Pierce

The boy lay on the edge of the pavement, spread-eagled on his back as if sleeping. But he wasn't sleeping. His ruined motorcycle, several feet away, turned on its side in the middle of the road, was proof of that.

*What could have caused this horrific accident?*

I stood at the boy's feet, staring at his bike, which has been pummeled and crushed far beyond repair. It was after midnight on a Tuesday, and I was alone at this eerie scene. There was no sign of human life anywhere for miles on this old back road. No headlights in the fog, no witnesses to answer my questions, several miles out of town on a road that looked seldom used.

I'd just moved here a few days before and hadn't found a job yet. I'd been at the local gay bar, meeting some of the locals, trying to make friends. Knowing I had to drive I drank soda only. At about midnight I'd said good-bye and got in my truck and headed to my new home. But somewhere along the line I'd taken a wrong turn and ended up on that desolate road in the middle of nowhere on a foggy night.

When my headlights picked out the shapes in the road ahead I pulled the truck to a stop and got out. As soon as I saw it was an accident I tried to call 911 on my cell, but for some reason there was no service available. I thought for sure I'd paid my bill, but there was no time to worry about that now. I knelt over the boy, searching for blood or obvious wounds, but found none. What I did find was that he was shockingly beautiful in a wild, animalistic way. His features were sharp and feral, like a wild child from a fairy tale. He was probably nineteen or twenty, wearing a dirty white T-shirt, torn jeans and black leather boots. He was very slender, skinny almost. I didn't see a helmet—maybe it had been knocked off in the crash?

But what had he crashed into?

There was nothing around that I could see—maybe it was a hit-and-run. Anger flared in me at the thought of someone doing this and then just leaving this boy and his bike in the middle of the road, not even knowing if he was alive or dead. I put my ear to his chest and heard the beat of his heart and felt the movement of his breathing. He was alive! I knew it was dangerous to move a wounded person but I didn't care. I was on my own and had to get this guy to safety. As gently as I could, I gathered the boy in my arms and picked him up off the pavement. He was very light. I carried him to my truck and put him in the passenger seat, then covered him with a blanket and pulled the shoulder harness across him, fastening him in nice and tight. After I was satisfied that he was secure, I had an argument with myself about the bike.

I finally decided that saving the boy's life was more important than preserving evidence from a crime scene, so I just dragged the remains of the motorcycle off the road and left them there instead of trying to bring them with us. I got back in the truck and did a U-turn, heading back the way I'd come. The whole time not one other car had appeared. I hoped heading back I would see something familiar and reorient myself.

The boy sat in the passenger seat, his head hanging forward, still out cold. Luckily the fog started clearing and soon enough I started recognizing landmarks and not long after that, I knew where we were. I thought about driving the wild child to the hospital but something told me not to, to take him home with me instead. Somehow, it was like I didn't want to share him with anyone else yet. I sort of felt like he was my responsibility.

Or like he was mine, period.

Soon enough I would have to give him up—to police, to doctors—and I wanted a little time with him that was just mine. None of these thoughts seemed strange at the time, although they do now. Something about that night, and the boy himself, was making me act and feel differently than normal.

I took him home with me to my little house.

I pulled the truck into my one-car garage and shut the door behind me. Carefully I unfastened the boy's safety belt and got him out of the truck onto his feet. Still unconscious, he sagged in my arms. He couldn't stand up, much less walk. I leaned over and let the biker boy fall over my left shoulder. I put my arms around his legs and gently picked him up, then closed the truck's door. I switched off the garage light behind us.

I carried him over my shoulder through the access door and down the hall, past the tiny kitchen and bathroom, into my small bedroom. Holding him in place over my shoulder with one hand, I used the other to toss aside the piles of dirty clothes on the bed. I laid him down on the bedspread, but before I could stand up he scared the piss out of me by grabbing at me with both arms.

"Fuck!" I cursed in surprise.

"Fuck..." he repeated. "Fuck...me."

I tried to pull away but he wouldn't let go.

"No!" he cried. "Don't leave me..."

"Are you hurt?" I asked, feeling more than a little freaked out. "Do you need me to take you to the hospital?"

The boy shook his head, his eyes opening into slits.

"No!" he said, "I need you to fuck me!"

"This is crazy," I said, "you were just in an accident..."

"FUCK ME!" he screamed in my face. The words were English but the sound was a noise an animal would make. I found it terrifying and arousing in a scary way. His hands shot down to my pants, clawing at them, scrabbling like a creature trying to escape a trap.

I don't know what came over me—the whole night had been so fucking weird—but I found myself answering his demented passion with some of my own. With both hands I sunk my fingers into the fabric of his dirty tee and tore the flimsy shirt apart. He hissed in appreciation as his slender, sinewy chest was revealed, his eyes watching me unblinkingly. By this time he'd yanked the buttons of my pants open and reached inside. I snarled as his clutching hand closed around my cock, which had gone from soft to stiff in record time. I dropped down on top of him, my greater weight pushing him into the mattress. I straddled him, working my way up his torso until my hard cock was flopping in his face. His mouth opened greedily but I grabbed my dick and held it away.

"You want it?" I yelled at him.

"Yes," he said breathlessly, "yes!"

"Then beg for it!" I spat at him. "Beg, bitch!"

His eyes glittered at me, almost reptilian in their cold hard glory.

"Fuck my mouth, please!" he begged. "Stick it in me, you

know you want to, fuck my mouth, fuck my mouth, fuck my—"

"Shut up!" I growled at him, shoving my now-dripping cock between his lips. He immediately started sucking like a baby at a teat. Within seconds my tool was dripping with the saliva he'd slathered it with. I pulled out of his mouth, and the boy moaned like a kid whose favorite toy had been taken away. He whined louder and I smacked him hard across his face.

"*Shut up!*" I roared. "You're *mine* now!"

Again this aggression, so different from my usual intimate manner, seemed perfectly normal at the time. I put my hands under his torso and easily flipped him over onto his stomach. Seizing the back of his jeans, I tore them down far enough to give me access to his asshole. In the dim light from the hallway I saw the pale skin of his back. Right above the cleft of his ass he had something tattooed. It was a circle, with many rays spreading out from its center, the outer border black and thick... I suddenly realized it was a motorcycle wheel, and the rays were spokes.

I spat on my hand and took my cock in my fist, aiming it for his hole. I pushed it against his pucker, and I felt it open, like he'd been waiting for this, like he wanted this badly, like he *needed* it...

"Fuck me!" he cried out. "Oh, fuck me, fuck me, fuck me—"

With all my strength I forced myself into him and let the weight of my torso settle on his back. I clapped my left hand over his mouth but he continued to moan and scream like an animal. The muffled noises he made seemed to change—from passion, to relief, to despair and grief...I ignored them and fucked him harder than I'd ever fucked a guy before, steadying myself with my right hand on the bed.

The boy bucked against me, his asshole pulling and sucking me farther and farther in like he wanted to be fucked by my whole body, not just my cock. The intensity crested and I climaxed, shooting my load deep into his guts. Finally his moaning quieted, until he was groaning and yelping softly under me. I pulled out of his ass and rolled over onto my back. He moved as if to get up but I grabbed him, as he had grabbed me. Now I was the one holding him, not letting him leave. He moaned in protest, but as I held him and stroked his head with one hand he soon relaxed and let me gather him in my arms. We fell asleep that way, my chest slowly heaving with long deep breaths, and the wild child breathing quickly like a small animal, a rabbit or a dog.

The next morning he was gone.

I had no memory of him leaving, but when I woke up I was clutching pillows. The bed was trashed, so obviously I'd fucked *something* the night before.... I sluggishly got up and turned on my little TV and logged onto my email account. I checked the local news and found nothing about a motorcycle accident.

Had I dreamed it?

Nothing that intense could have been created by my imagination. My cock was sore for one thing, and not from my hand. It had been no wet dream, there was no stain on my bed. What the fuck had happened?

I got dressed and went to town, looking for work. I got a few leads, nothing definite. That night I went to the same gay bar, said hello to a few friendly faces. The bartender, a good-looking guy himself, looked at me and grinned.

"Didn't get much sleep last night?" he asked with a knowing look. Against my better judgment, I told him a quick version of what I'd experienced the night before. He seemed very interested in what I thought was a trivial detail—the boy's tattoo. He called some of the other customers over and fixed me with a serious face.

"Spokeboy paid him a visit last night," he told them. The

other guys nodded slowly, as if they knew exactly what he was talking about.

"What the hell?" I asked. The bartender got me a new drink.

"About five years ago this motorcycle kid who hung out here—everyone called him 'spokeboy' 'cause of his tattoo—he got dumped by his boyfriend, a real son-of-a-bitch biker dude. Real bad breakup, the kid was devastated. The biker just got on his bike and left, said he was never coming back. Spokeboy was crying and screaming, said he would follow him and make him take him back."

One of the other guys took up the story.

"Kid got on his bike. It was a real foggy night, we all tried to stop him but he fought us off. He took off and never came back. Next morning we found out that a few miles out of town he'd had a head-on with a semi. He must've been driving stupid, not paying attention. He was killed instantly, it was a hit-and-run. They never found the semi driver."

I put my drink down and stared at the guys, looking for deception, humor, anything—but there was nothing there, except maybe sadness.

"Apparently spokeboy lay out there on the road for several hours before a cop car drove by. And ever since then, well, we don't laugh when someone comes in and tells us about this hit-and-run accident they came across a few miles out of town. Or when they tell us they took the boy with the bike wheel tattoo home and he begged them to fuck him."

"No, we don't laugh at all," the other guy said.

The bartender put his hand on my shoulder.

"Welcome to the neighborhood," he said.

# MEAT AND POTATOES

Michael Bracken

I shot the lying motherfucker fifteen times. I had to reload twice to do it, and I would have continued shooting Thompson if I hadn't run out of bullets.

When my ears stopped ringing, I heard a polite cough. That's when I realized someone was standing behind me. My rock-hard cock instantly shriveled.

I turned and found myself facing a bald-headed behemoth whose thick, muscular arms were covered in black and blue tattoos of no discernible pattern. He wore scuffed black motorcycle boots, faded blue jeans, and a sleeveless black T-shirt tight as a second skin. He held a sawed-off double-barrel shotgun in one hand and half a beignet in the other.

"You done yet?"

I swallowed hard and nodded.

"Then get out of the way."

I stepped aside and the man mountain emptied both barrels of the shotgun into Thompson's remains.

"I always wanted to do that," the behemoth said. He stuffed the last of the beignet into his mouth, broke the shotgun open, and reloaded. "Let's go."

"Where?"

"Any place but here, citizen," he said. "The cops'll be coming soon." I followed him out of Thompson's two-bedroom bungalow and, as we crossed the porch, he asked, "How'd you get here?"

"Thompson drove."

"Then I guess you'll need to ride with me." He led me down the steps and across the weed-choked lawn to a candy-apple red Harley-Davidson Shovelhead with ape-hanger handlebars and chopper forks leaning on its kickstand. After stuffing the sawed-off into a custom-made leather holster, he straddled the bike. "Mind riding bitch?"

I shook my head.

A moment later he kick-started the engine and the familiar *potato-potato-potato* Harley-Davidson sound filled my ears. I shoved Thompson's revolver into my jacket pocket, climbed on behind the behemoth and tried to wrap my arms around him. I couldn't. Then we were off, down the street and around the corner from the dead man's house.

I wore penny loafers, chinos and a polo shirt under my windbreaker. I hadn't bothered to retrieve my socks and I had no idea where my briefs had gone. I did have a wad of cash in my pants pocket, money I'd taken from Thompson's dresser before I'd shot him. The rumble of the motorcycle between my thighs gave me a rock-hard erection that rubbed against the inside of my chinos and pressed against the behemoth's lower back. If he noticed the pressure from my cock and the wad of bills, he didn't say anything.

But I probably couldn't have heard him if he had.

We rode across town, weaving in and out of traffic until we came to another neighborhood that might as well have been around the corner from the dead man's house for all the difference twenty miles made. We wheeled up onto the sidewalk in front of a ramshackle bungalow that might have once been painted white. The house had a wheelchair ramp extending from the porch to the sidewalk and he drove the Shovelhead straight up the ramp, stopping on the porch only long enough to unlock the front door and for us both to get off before he wheeled the bike into the living room and locked the door behind us.

My host wasn't big on decoration. The only things in the living room other than the Shovelhead were a red thirteen-drawer Craftsman tool cart on wheels, a flat-screen TV, and a black leather couch held together with gray duct tape and covered on one end by a black leather jacket with his motorcycle club's insignia on the back.

The man-mountain put one hand on my shoulder and propelled me down the hallway. "Take a shower, citizen. Try to wash the stink off."

I did as I was told, and when I stepped out of the shower twenty minutes later I discovered that my clothes were gone—my clothes and everything in my pockets. I wrapped a threadbare blue towel around my slim hips and walked through the house until I found my host sitting at the yellow Formica and chrome kitchen table, Thompson's revolver in pieces in front of him, the wad of Thompson's cash near his left elbow, and my wallet, keys and pocket change piled on my side of the table. My wallet was open and my driver's license stuck half out of it.

The behemoth had taken off his T-shirt, and I saw the word MEAT tattooed across his chest in six-inch-tall black Olde English script. I pointed at his chest.

"That your name?"

"Good as any other," he replied. He held up the disassembled revolver. "Where'd you get this?"

"In Thompson's nightstand, same as the bullets," I told him. "Where are my clothes?"

"Washing machine." He motioned toward the refrigerator. "Get me a beer. Get yourself one, too."

Inside the Frigidaire I found a half-empty twenty-four-pack of Dixie and pulled two cans from it. I returned to the table with a beer in each hand. When I put Meat's on the table in front of him I realized he hadn't just removed his T-shirt; he was butt-ass naked under the table.

"Where are *your* clothes?"

"With yours." As if to punctuate his statement, the sink drain gurgled and water from the washing machine began backing up into it.

Meat opened his beer, swallowed half the can, then finished cleaning the revolver and reassembled it. He watched me the entire time, taking his measure of me the way I was taking my measure of him.

"Got a little something for you," Meat said. He pushed back his chair and stood. My eyes widened in surprise. Many of the bulked-up men I'd been with were steroid abusers, with shriveled balls, limp dicks, and acne on their asses. Not Meat. He'd built his muscles the old-fashioned way, and his semierect cock was a one-eyed python rising from a tangled nest of black hair.

I licked my lips, wetting them with just the tip of my tongue. Worse than being a lying motherfucker, Thompson had been a terrible lay, barely able to sustain the pitiable little erection he'd managed even after I'd spent half an hour sucking like a Hoover, and I was still horny as a virgin on Viagra.

The threadbare towel fell away from my hips as I dropped to my knees on the linoleum floor and kissed the swollen head of

my host's cock, teasing his cum-slit with my tongue. I licked all
the way around the ridge of his glans and then used the tip of my
tongue to trace a wet line down the underside of his engorged
cock to his heavy ball sac. I sucked his nuts into my mouth
and sucked them hard, stretching his sac and collecting curly
black hair between my teeth. Then my tongue raced back up
the length of his cock and I took his cockhead into my mouth.
I swallowed more and more of it until I thought I couldn't take
any more. Meat thought different. He grabbed the back of my
head, his thick fingers threading through my blond hair, and
face-fucked me.

When he finally came, he came hard, and cum exploded
against the back of my throat. I couldn't swallow fast enough,
and some of it leaked from the corners of my mouth and down
my chin. As he stepped back, pulling his cock from my oral
cavity, I wiped my chin with the back of my hand.

He pulled me to my feet and propelled me down the hall
to the bedroom, which was as sparsely furnished as his living
room, with an unmade king-sized bed filling most of the available space. The nightstand held a lamp without a shade, a clock
radio and a half-used tube of lube. Three plastic clothes baskets
filled with folded clothing   underwear, T-shirts and socks
lined one wall. Dirty clothes were piled in one corner. The closet
door stood half open, and I could see the sawed-off in its holster
along with several handguns hanging from a pegboard mounted
to the back wall. Before I could crane my neck for a better
look at Meat's armory, he bent me over the side of the bed and
reached for his lube. He slathered the slick goo over his middle
finger and then began stroking my sphincter. I spread my legs,
opening my ass to his digital manipulation. He pressed the tip
of his finger against my anal opening and pushed. By the time
he had his finger buried to the first knuckle, my cock started to

rise. By the time he had his entire finger up my ass, my cock was hard as a rock.

Meat reached around, wrapped one fist around my cock, and began to pump so vigorously I thought he was going to snap my cock off. At the same time he was jerking me off, he was finger-fucking my ass, and after the fiasco with Thompson the previous evening I was glad to be with a real man.

Before I could stop myself—not that I wanted to—I came, spewing cum all over Meat's bedsheet. My legs turned to gelatin, and I thought my knees would buckle. Meat pulled his finger from my ass and grabbed my hips to keep me upright. The python between his legs had awoken again, and he pressed his cockhead against my butt pucker. He had prepped me, lubing my hole quite thoroughly and stretching my opening with his thick finger, but I wasn't truly prepared for what came next.

He drove his long, thick cock into my ass and didn't stop until every last bit of it was inside me. He drew back until only his cockhead remained inside, and then he drove forward again. He held my hips so tight he left ten fingertip-sized bruises that I didn't notice until later. I also didn't notice the pain of his tight grip because my attention was fully concentrated on the pain and pleasure of the ass-fucking I was getting. He thrust savagely for a full five minutes, time I watched count down on the clock radio, and then he fired a load nearly as voluminous as the one he'd popped in my mouth.

He held me until his cock stopped spasming, and then he pulled away and let me drop face-first on the dirty sheet. He left me there and disappeared into the bathroom. When he returned, he threw a damp washcloth—the one I'd used earlier to clean off cordite and Thompson's blood—and told me to clean up.

After Meat moved our clothes from the washing machine to the dryer, we returned to the kitchen still naked, opened two more Dixies and a sack of day-old beignets, and sat at the yellow Formica and chrome table where we'd sat before we'd fucked.

After downing half his beer, Meat asked, "Why'd you shoot Thompson?"

"He promised me two hundred for the night. Then he refused to pay."

"So you took his money and shot him?" He retrieved a beignet from the bag.

"Yeah."

"How many times?"

"Fifteen."

"Once would have been enough."

I shrugged.

"Why'd *you* shoot him?"

"Seemed like a good idea at the time." He shoved the beignet into his mouth, chewed, and swallowed.

"Why were you even there?"

"I'm the MC's sergeant at arms," Meat explained. "The club's enforcer. If somebody doesn't do something they're supposed to do, I remind them of their responsibilities. Thompson was behind in his dues." He licked confectioner's sugar off one thick finger—the same finger he'd had up my ass—and used it to nudge the wad of bills I'd taken from Thompson's dresser. "Looks like he was holding out on us."

"You ever kill anybody?"

The behemoth sat up straight as if to remind me of his imposing physique. "Never needed to."

I looked a question at him.

"Thompson was the first guy I ever shot," he said, "but I'm pretty sure he was already dead when I arrived."

Thompson wasn't the first guy I'd ever shot, but I didn't tell Meat that.

He peeled a pair of Benjamins off the roll and tossed them at me. "Here's what Thompson owes you," he said. "The rest goes to the club."

I put the Benjamins in my wallet and pushed my driver's license back into place. Then I stood. "Think my clothes are dry?"

"You planning to leave?"

"Might as well." I held up my wallet. "I got what I wanted."

"Don't do anything stupid after you leave here, Kyle," Meat threatened. "I know where you live."

He had seen my driver's license, but it didn't matter. It was a forgery. "I haven't lived there in years."

"Yeah?" he said. "Where do you live?"

"Around," I said. "Here and there. Depends."

"Depends on how many tricks you turn?"

I shrugged. I let him think he'd nailed it.

"I could use somebody around here," he said. "You looking for something steady?"

"Sure," I told him. "Why not?"

I could ride bitch for a day or a week or a month or a year. Sooner or later I'd figure out where the big motherfucker kept his money and where he kept his ammo and how soundly he slept. And with all those guns in his closet I could do more than shoot him fifteen times. I'd let him fuck me until I was ready to fuck him over.

I smiled at the thought. Bikers were so easy.

Meat thought I was smiling at him and he took me back to the bedroom.

# TAKEN

## Wayne Mansfield

The horizon was growing darker. The fiery glow of another sunset had been eaten up by the oncoming night. I looked at my car's fuel gauge and hoped I would find a petrol station before nightfall because if I didn't, I was in for either a long night or a long walk. Neither prospect delighted me. Trees and paddocks went whizzing by as I planted my foot on the accelerator. I was way over the speed limit but didn't care, I'd rather pay a fifty buck fine than the cost of a tow truck.

Suddenly the twilight was filled with the roar of motorcycles. I looked up at my rearview mirror. At first I couldn't see anything, but then the road was awash with the lights of about three dozen bikes. I kept my eye on the bikers, slowing to let them pass. They roared past me, not one of them looking at me as they sped by on their Harley-Davidsons and Ducatis.

*Thank god for that,* I thought.

It must have been a quarter of an hour later when I saw a sign for a petrol station and diner up ahead. I looked at my fuel gauge and saw it was almost at the zero mark.

"Come on, come on!" I muttered, willing the car to keep going until I reached the station. I think my Toyota made the last mile on fumes alone, but make it I did. The trouble was, the bikers had arrived before me. I could see them inside the diner, a mass of denim and leather, plaid shirts and tattoos. I kept my eyes on them as I stood at the pump filling my car. I'd always had a fantasy of being taken by a group of bikers, or a team of football players, but fantasy doesn't always translate well into reality. I hated to admit it but I was more afraid than turned on.

The handle on the nozzle clicked off and I hung it back up. I shut and locked the lid of my fuel tank and walked across the dirt to the diner. As I got to the door I swallowed hard and pushed it open. Immediately I had three dozen eyes on me. I smiled weakly and walked across to the counter, trying my damndest not to make eye contact with any of them.

A rather voluptuous brunette with thick eyeliner and tobacco-stained teeth came out of the kitchen with two plates in her hand. She looked about forty-five and wore a stained white uniform that was about as low-cut as you could get and still call it a uniform. The buttons strained trying to contain a set of the biggest tits I'd ever seen.

"Steak and veg," she called out, her voice sounding flat and uninterested. "Repeat. Two steak and veg."

One of the bikers walked over, threw a twenty onto the counter and grabbed the plates out of her hands.

"Like to give ya me tube steak, love," he said, his voice deep and rough.

The waitress snatched the twenty off the counter.

"That'll cost ya a lot more than a twenty, lover," she deadpanned.

"How much then?" he asked.

The waitress rang up the sale on the cash register, looked at him and closed her eyes.

"More than you could ever hope to raise," she said, opening her eyes again.

A few of the biker's mates laughed, and he decided to quit while he was ahead.

"The offer is open, sexy," he said. "Think about it."

The waitress came shuffling toward me.

"I promise you, it'll be all I think about!" she said over her shoulder. "Now, what'll it be for you?"

"I just got some petrol," I replied.

"Which number?"

"One, I think. Thirty dollars."

She pushed some buttons on a second cash register and took the fifty I handed her. She gave me my change, and I asked her where the toilets were. She nodded to my right and started walking down to the other end of the counter. I called out my thank-you and headed off for the men's room. I'd planned to get in and out as fast as possible, but nature was making a sudden and desperate call which I had no choice but to answer.

I pushed the wooden door open and then a second inner door. The toilet was dimly lit and stank of stale piss and urinal cakes. I scanned the room and found that thankfully I was alone. I debated whether to use a cubicle or the urinal but after glancing into the first stall and seeing what someone had left there I decided upon the urinal.

I stepped up to the trough, unzipped my jeans and fished out my flaccid cock. I'd just started to piss when I heard the door behind me open. *Shit!* I thought. From the corner of my eye I saw someone step right up next to me. I frowned. I hated it when someone did that, especially when the rest of the trough was free.

I glanced sideways, as surreptitiously as I could, and saw that it was one of the bikers. The smell of cigarette smoke and leather was strong on him. While my eyes were there I couldn't help but sneak a peek at his cock, but I could only see the hood of his uncut prick.

"Why don't you take a good look?" he said in a voice that was masculine and commanding.

I nearly shat myself. My eyes stared straight ahead and my lips stayed firmly shut, hoping he'd leave me alone. I willed myself to piss faster so I could shake myself dry and get the fuck out of there.

"Go on," he said. "You wanna see it so bad. Take a good look at it."

I looked at the man: six feet of solid muscle. He was wearing a blue tank top, denim jeans and leather chaps. His boots had thick soles and black laces, probably steel-capped too.

And then I saw his face.

I glanced away, thinking he was the hottest thing I'd seen in a long time. His eyes were so green they dazzled like emeralds, even in the pale fluorescent light of the bathroom. He had jet-black buzz-cut hair and a small goatee. His teeth were perfectly white, stark against the dark lips that were smiling at me.

His beautiful eyes looked down and I followed them to his cock, which was now much bigger than it had been when I looked before. He was shaking the last few drops of piss from it, using long, slow strokes. The foreskin that had been covering his reddish-pink cockhead was slowly receding as the biker's prick continued to harden.

"I saw you coming in," he said. "I thought you might be into cock."

My heart was pounding. I could feel that my own dick had become erect and now jutted out of my open fly like a javelin. I glanced nervously over my shoulder at the door.

"Don't worry," he said. "They're too busy eating and drinking."

He reached down and grabbed my cock. His touch was electric as I felt the warmth of his hand flood my body. I grabbed his prick and together we started jerking each other off.

"Nice cock," he said, giving it a squeeze.

I continued tugging on his steel-hard dick, looking into his eyes and wanting more than anything to kiss those full lips. He must have seen me looking at his mouth because at that very instant he brought his tongue to his top lip and held it there. I looked him in the eye and he held my stare.

In the heat of the moment I leaned forward and pressed my lips against him. To my amazement he reciprocated, his lips soft beneath mine, his breath warm and fragrant in my mouth.

He bent down and took the head of my cock in his mouth and started sucking it. I closed my eyes and put my hands on his bristly head, pulling it deeper onto my cock. His mouth was warm and wet around the firmness of my shaft, and I could feel his tongue slithering over and around it, then probing my piss-slit. I moaned a soft long sigh of release as the biker took my cock down the very back of his throat.

I was so caught up in the rhythmic motion of his mouth on my prick I didn't feel him reach around behind me. The next thing I knew there was a finger at my arsehole, pressing against it, demanding to enter. I pushed back and did my best to relax my sphincter muscle. Soon he was able to drive his finger in through the tight band of muscle to the soft, damp cavern on the other side.

I groaned, the sigh falling off my parted lips. The smell of the restroom, the noises coming from the dining room and the sense of danger all worked upon my senses. Opening my eyes for a moment to look at the he-man sucking me off at the edge of the piss-reeking urinal, I felt my balls tighten.

I was breathing in short, sharp bursts. My hips began thrusting into his mouth, wanting more of me inside him. His nose poked into my thick thatch of curly dark blond pubic hair as his mouth slid up and down my hard cock.

"Oh, fuck, I'm gonna come," I whispered as quietly as I could, which wasn't that quietly. "I'm gonna fucking blow."

The biker amped up the pace, his mouth like a Hoover on my prick. His finger wriggled inside me, massaging my rock-hard prostate. Finally I blew. I knew it was a big load because I could see it dribbling out through the corners of his mouth, and I could feel jet after jet rocketing out of my swollen cockhead. But his tongue! Holy shit, his tongue! It kept flicking over the head of my cock, making my whole body shudder. My abdominal muscles kept contracting, even though the cum supply had been used up. I felt the firm tip of his tongue probe my piss-slit, licking out one last drop of pearly white man-cream.

Then we heard the sound of a door opening. My heart jumped into my throat, stopping the flow of oxygen. I felt my cheeks burn red as I turned and pretended I was still pissing. Beside me the biker leapt to his feet and pretended to do the same.

"You've been in here a long time, Jakey mate," said the new arrival.

"Didn't know you were timing me, buddy," said Jake with a small laugh that made him sound guilty. The other biker went into one of the cubicles. I guess being a biker, nothing fazed him.

"Meet me out the front. We'll go somewhere," Jake whispered to me.

All I could do was nod. My eyes were glued to the shut cubicle door. I washed my hands and dried them as quickly as I could while Jake hovered behind me.

"You mind if I bring a couple of mates?" he asked.

I shook my head and hurried past him.

The cool night air felt soothing against my face. I rushed over to my car and only then did I stop and take a deep breath. Inside, through the windows, I could see the other bikers becoming raucous; one of them pinched the waitress's bottom and got a slap for his troubles. I suddenly felt sorry for her, having to put up with that all the time.

I waited and waited for Jake to come out, the whole time debating whether or not I should just get in my car and drive off. I had already blown my load. What was there to stay for? While I found Jake attractive, there was no telling what his mates were like. Finally, I decided to leave. He'd obviously forgotten about me anyway. I unlocked my car door and got in, started the engine and put it into gear. The car rolled forward and only then did I see Jake leaping down the stairs and running toward me. I almost didn't recognize him since he was wearing his leather jacket now. I pressed my foot on the brake.

"What are you doing, mate?" he asked. "I told ya to wait for me."

I suddenly felt like a prize arsehole.

"Sorry. I thought you'd forgotten about me."

"Mate, how could I forget about ya? I can't just grab me buddies and leave, ya know. Took me a while to think of an excuse. I told them we'd meet them up the road a bit, in Sutton's Creek. There's a pub there with rooms. We get a discount there."

"So what are we gonna do?" I asked. "You want me to follow you somewhere?"

"No, mate. Park ya car over there in the parking lot. I'll take you on my bike and drop ya off again when we've finished."

I balked at his offer. I didn't really want to be stranded out here in the bush away from my car.

He seemed to sense my hesitance.

"You'll be fine. Look, I'll leave ya me license. You can put it in ya car and I'll pick it up when I drop ya off."

That sounded like a fair deal, so I parked my car, took his license and threw it into the glove box, then followed him over to his bike.

"Put this on," he said, thrusting a helmet into my hands.

While I was doing up the strap I took a look at his two friends. One was older, maybe forty-five. He had gray hair and a thick beard. His leather jacket didn't conceal the slight potbelly he had. The other guy was about thirty-six, thirty-seven and was tall and solidly built. He was hairy too, even his hands were hairy. He had a mustache and goatee, and lots of piercings. I liked the look of him.

"This is Tab. His mother used to get moist over Tab Hunter," Jake said pointing to the older guy, who extended his hand for me to shake. "And this one here is Luke."

I shook both their hands and then Luke asked me what my name was.

"Ryan," I replied.

Luke ran a finger over my lips, pushing it into my mouth.

"Well, you're a pretty one, Ryan," he said. "I'm getting hard just thinking about fucking you."

He grabbed his crotch and I could see that he was telling the truth. If he'd looked down at *my* crotch he would've seen that I was just as hard. The three bikers got on their hogs and I threw my leg over Jake's bike, clambering on behind him.

"Hold tight," he said.

I said I would, but my reply was drowned out by the noise of the motorcycle engines starting up. In seconds we were out of there, a trail of dust spiraling into the night behind us. The wind against my face was exhilarating. I'd never been on a bike before, having always thought they were too dangerous, but I was really enjoying the sense of freedom the bike gave me—it was something a car couldn't provide. The moonlit countryside was a blur as we sped down the highway. I felt laughter building up in the pit of my stomach but I swallowed it down. I didn't want to look like an amateur, even though everyone knew I was.

Finally we turned off the main highway onto a dirt track. We only went a mile or so along it before we came to a clearing in the trees and shrubbery.

The silence seemed strange after the roar of the engines. The bikers climbed off their rides and removed their helmets, hanging them on their handlebars. I followed their lead and when I turned around Luke was right behind me.

"You sure are a pretty one," he said again. "I love blonds."

I was twenty-six, much younger than any of them. I was five nine and my body was toned and naturally smooth, though there was a line of fine hair in the crack of my arse and the hair around my seven-inch cock was thick. I had light brown eyes and, yes, my hair was dark blond.

"Let's take it over here a bit," said Jake. "There's some grass down by the creek. It'll be more comfortable."

I saw Luke frown in the moonlight.

"Just make it quick," he growled. "I got a week's worth of jizz to blow up his tight cunt."

Jake squatted down, grabbed me around the waist and threw me over his shoulder. I hung there like something that had been hunted. His shoulder was boring into my belly and my nostrils were filled with the smell of his leather jacket. Then he farted. I screwed my nose up as I got my first whiff of it.

"That was one I didn't want," he said with a smile in his voice.

We pushed through the undergrowth, and I was suddenly

worried that I would never see the light of day again. I knew his license was in my car but what was to stop him from doing away with me and then breaking into my car to get it back? I'd been a complete idiot, but I guessed it was too late to do anything about it now. I'd just have to watch myself.

I was thrown gently down into the long grass. It was soft and cushioned my back nicely.

"Let's get his clothes off," said Luke, bending down and undoing the button to my jeans. The others didn't speak but started pulling my clothing off until I was completely naked. Underneath the light of a full moon I felt exposed and vulnerable. The three bikers were still fully clothed and were standing over me, looking down at my hard cock.

"Let's wash him down first," said Tab, unzipping his fly. "No telling where a pretty boy like him's been."

All three took their cocks out, aimed them at me and then emptied their bladders. Their piss was warm against the cool evening air, and I had to admit it was turning me on. Three streams of golden liquid covered me completely, from my feet to my face. I even swallowed some, the liquid salty on my tongue with a slightly acrid aftertaste.

When they had finished shaking the last drops from their piss-slits, Luke knelt down and grabbed my legs. He pushed them up into the air, spreading them wide so my arsehole was stretched open. He looked at it for a couple of seconds and then speared into it with his tongue. I felt the ring of muscle contract around his tongue then loosen as he licked it.

"You got a sweet arse, boy," he said between licks.

"I'll be fucked if I let him have all the fun,' said Tab, undoing his belt buckle and letting his jeans drop down to his ankles. I watched as he shuffled over to me, turned around and squatted down over my face.

"Now eat my hairy arse, son," he told me.

I could smell it before it touched my face. It wasn't an unpleasant smell, just earthy, musty. And it was very hairy. I felt his arse hair touch my face before his arsehole did. My tongue went straight to work, poking at his hole and licking it. I sucked on his arse-lips like I was kissing him, using my tongue to push against the ring of muscle beneath all that hair. He sat down harder, making it difficult for me to breathe. I was forced to draw in air through my nose and with it came the funky aroma of his sweaty arsehole. It was all I could smell and with each breath my cock twitched. It was a smell that had always turned me on.

I didn't know what Jake was doing. I couldn't see anything but a set of full, hairy balls. Tab was grinding his arsehole into my mouth and jerking off. I could feel his heavy nuts bouncing on my forehead. Behind him I felt Luke ease me to the ground. His tongue had left my hole, but it was only seconds before it had been replaced by something more substantial: his cock. I yelped when he pushed the head of his fat nine-incher into my barely lubricated arsehole, but my cry of pain went unheard, muffled by Tab's hairy hole.

After a few seconds my anal muscles relaxed and the discomfort of having something so thick and long up there became pleasurable. Luke began thrusting, deep and slow, easing into me while he adjusted his hands on my legs. His fingers around my knees were firm. I could feel the power in his arms and now that he had me where he wanted me he began to pump faster and harder.

"Got a tight hole, this one," he said.

I listened for a response but there wasn't one. Instead I saw Jake take position in front of Tab, his pants off though he was still wearing his tank top and jacket. His beautiful cock slid into Tab's mouth, and I was suddenly jealous that it wasn't my mouth he was fucking. I watched over and around Tab's bouncing dick, loving the way he sucked Jake's cock slowly into his mouth and then eased it out again, nothing hurried about it. I felt my own cock twitch and wondered how soon it would be before someone took care of it. I had already come once that night, but I was well and truly ready to go again.

Shortly after he started sucking Jake's thick prick, Tab began to jerk his own meat. His balls slapped and danced on my forehead in an annoyingly irregular way. He grunted and puffed as he sucked Jake's cock and sometimes sat down a little too hard on my face. My arms were free so I was able to push him off enough for me to be able to breathe.

Luke became more vocal. I could hear him over Tab's nasal breaths, grunting and puffing as though he were ready to blow. He was certainly hammering my hole. My hard cock was slapping against my flat stomach in time to the thrusting of his hips, splattering precum all over my torso and pubes. His balls were also slapping against the hairy skin of my groin, sticking there slightly with sweat before being peeled off again by the motion of his fucking. I spread my legs wider for him and willed him to shoot his load. I wanted to feel him unload deep inside my guts, to know that I had his weeks' worth of jizz inside me.

And then it happened. Luke let out a loud cry and slammed into me so hard it almost dislodged Tab from my face.

"Fuckin' hell!" he cried out as his cock unleashed a powerful gush of cum into me. "Fuckin' hell!"

Tab quickened the pace on his cock. Soon he was grunting too, and I knew he'd blown his load across the grass. As he shuddered the last few drops of his cock-cream rained down on my face and ran backward into my hair.

"Did ya come?" I heard Jake ask him.

"Sure did," he replied as he wiped his cock on my forehead. I heard his knee crack as he stood up. He groaned and muttered something about getting old.

Luke stayed inside me for a while, leaning forward over me on his arms. I looked at him now that the way was clear and smiled. He frowned back and my smile evaporated. Nevertheless, he was careful when he pulled his deflating cock out and for that at least I was grateful; a weapon that size could do damage.

"My turn," said Jake.

The moment I'd been waiting for. From the minute I'd first seen his cock in the men's restroom I'd wanted to feel it inside me. I never thought I would until he asked me to meet him outside the diner and only then did I imagine it could happen.

Jake settled between my legs and looked down at me. I wasn't sure but I thought I saw him wink at me. He lifted my legs, resting my right leg on his shoulder as he guided his cock into my sloppy hole. His cock slid in effortlessly, because of the thick load Luke had deposited there, and even squelched a little when he started thrusting.

I couldn't take my eyes off him as he fucked me. He kept his attention on me as well. He reached down and took my hand and placed it on my hard cock. I guessed he was giving me permission to pleasure myself. I was only too happy to accommodate. My cock was so hard and so sensitive I had to take it slowly. I wanted my climax to coincide with his.

Luke reappeared out of nowhere. He squatted down over my face and shoved his still semihard cock into my mouth. As the tip of it touched my lips I screwed my face up. It had been up my arse, after all.

"Suck it, slut!" he said, pushing it against my lips. "Open that slut mouth and suck my cock."

I didn't have any choice. I opened up and let him feed his

cock into my mouth. I started sucking it, running my tongue over it. I wanted to do the best job I could since Luke was a bit of a wild card. I didn't want to piss him off, and I didn't know if I could depend on Jake to protect me or not.

"That's it, little slut, suck that fat cock clean," Luke said.

I kept sucking, even though I was concentrating on the way Jake's cock felt sliding in and out of my tight hole. His hands were firm but gentle around my legs, and I loved the feeling of my smooth buttcheeks against his hairy thighs, scratchy and rough. He was all man and I couldn't wait until he emptied his balls into me.

Finally Luke got up. He pulled his pants up, buttoned them, then disappeared behind me for a smoke. I could smell it clearly, polluting the fresh night air.

I felt my balls tighten and the familiar sensation of climax start to build. I slid my fingers along my shaft and pinched my cock just behind the head. I didn't want to come until Jake did, I'd already decided that, and watched his face for any signs that he was going to blow his load. I liked the way he pursed his lips and how the ligaments in his throat became taut when he thrust into me.

I grabbed my cock again.

"You want my load, Ryan?" Jake asked. "You want Jake to empty his balls into that sweet arse?"

I nodded.

"Say it," he said.

"I want your load, Jake. I've wanted it all night."

He seemed turned on by that thought and began thrusting deeper and faster.

"Your big biker cock feels so good inside me," I said. "Give me that load. I wanna feel your cock go off inside me. Come on, Jake. Give it to me!"

He looked at me for a while longer. His grip on my legs tightened and his hips began to jackhammer me, pushing his perfect cock deeper and deeper. Then I saw him grimace. He gritted his teeth and grunted through them.

"Here it comes," he spat. "Here it fuckin' comes!"

He opened his mouth and cried out. I felt the first surge of cum hit my bowels and then nothing as the rest of his load fountained into my guts. He pushed his cock right into me, keeping it there and grinding his hips into my groin. I felt the sweat from his brow splatter my thighs and stomach. Just as his thrusts started to slow I shot my own load, a great streak of sticky man-cream that landed in a nearly straight line across my torso, from the base of my neck to the top of my pubic bush.

"How was that?" he asked, smiling down at me.

"Fuckin' hot," I replied. There was no other way to describe it.

Jake leaned down and kissed me, his thick lips brushing against mine, tasting, sensing, before parting to take my top lip between his. His kisses were tender, just a few lingering pecks before he pulled himself out of me and stood up.

"You two lovebirds finished yet?" shouted Luke. "We gotta get to Sutton's Creek."

"Well, don't let me hold ya up," said Jake. "I'm gonna take Ryan back to his car."

The other two threw their cigarette butts into the water and walked back past Jake and me. Tab looked down at me and smiled but Luke didn't acknowledge me at all. It didn't bother me. I'd never see either of them again.

Jake was as good as his word. As Tab and Luke started their bikes and took off into the night, Jake and I got dressed. We climbed onto his bike and raced back to the diner, now shrouded in darkness. I climbed off his bike, took the helmet off and handed it back to him.

"Thanks," I said. I wanted to say more but what more was there to say? It was what it was—one hell of a quick fuck.

"I had a good time too," he said. Then he paused. "Shit, my license!"

I pulled my car keys out of my jeans pocket and unlocked my car. I grabbed his license and walked back over to him. I handed him the license and he took it, his fingers wrapping around my hand. He pulled me to him and we kissed again.

"I really did enjoy myself," he said. "You look after yourself."

I nodded and stepped back as he revved his bike up and took off in a cloud of dust that stung my eyes.

"You too," I said, as I watched him disappear into the night.

# HARD RIDE

Dale Chase

Everything about him looked new and it made me want to pull him off his motorcycle, get him down in the dirt and fuck him. As it was, the traffic light changed and he took off, leaving me trapped inside my rental car.

I followed, of course, looking at an ass inside too-bright jeans, at desert boots that had never seen a grain of sand, and a shiny leather jacket with a row of racing checks from shoulder to shoulder. It was cut narrow at the waist and accented a back that funneled down into slim hips. Even his helmet glistened. I was getting hard just driving behind him and I thought about that, driving behind him all right, shoving my stiff prick up that sweet ass.

Part of the attraction undoubtedly had to do with circumstance, me trapped in a business suit for a week of fourteen-hour days hammering out contracts. All I wanted now was to hammer some ass and here it was in front of me, astride a great thundering beast. I kept my eyes on the rider. He was invisible inside his gear but had me anyway, and I fixed on little else as we sped north on Sepulveda Boulevard.

It was Thursday morning, a gorgeous summer day, and I was headed toward the rental car return at the Los Angeles airport, due back in San Francisco at noon. Suddenly I found myself reconsidering, and when I reached my turn I let it go by. Crossing the intersection brought a wonderful release. To hell with airlines and San Francisco and the rest of it. I meant to have this guy.

Once past the airport we cut over to Lincoln Boulevard, then headed out toward the beach and were soon doubling back along Pacific Coast Highway. A nice drive in any case, better with a throbbing hard-on and prey in my sights. As we made our way south, I started to notice that the motorcycle wasn't one of those garish speed machines that always seemed to be cutting me off in traffic. No, this one was the old-fashioned kind where the rider sits up straight. It was what motorcycles were before they got hijacked by Day-Glo paint. The fact that this guy hadn't succumbed to flash made him all the more appealing.

He led me to Manhattan Beach and when he turned up through numbered streets I followed, certain he was now well aware he'd scored. He pulled up at the rear of a large two-story Spanish-style house and I stopped across the alley.

Without so much as a glance my way he unlocked the garage, and I contented myself with a first look at the entire connection. I had my hand at my crotch and felt the familiar surge that makes me want to take whatever is nearby. Once the garage was open, the biker went inside and turned toward me, taking off his helmet, revealing tousled brown hair and a boyish grin. I got out of the car and crossed to him.

"Nice bike," I said, not looking at it. His eyes were almost black, eyelashes thick, cheeks flushed from the ride.

"I've only had it a couple of months," he said. "It's really hot." He reached down and adjusted his package and that did it. I hit the garage door button and by the time it closed, I had my dick out, aimed and ready.

He eyed it and smiled but when he started to take off his jacket I told him no. "Just the pants."

He complied, getting naked from the waist down and presenting me with a short, thick plug of cock.

"Want to go inside?" he asked and I shook my head. I had my pants down now and I pushed him onto the concrete floor beside the motorcycle. Looking at him on all fours, pink butt at the ready, I sucked in the heat of an engine mixed with the scent of a ready ass. The combination was intoxicating.

Despite appearances, his bottom was far from pristine and I savored a bittersweet taste as I licked his rim, then pushed my tongue into his hole. He had his hand on his cock as I fed at his ass and lubed him with spit.

When I withdrew it was only to move from tongue to cock, his pucker blinking at me, beckoning as if it couldn't stand being left alone, and then I did it, got a condom on in record time, got my swollen prong into him in one long sweet stroke. As I began a mighty thrust, the biker let out a yell and started coming.

He kept pumping cream as I kept pumping ass and he got more and more vocal as I did him. Instead of going quiet when he was empty, he picked up speed, and I realized I'd found one of those wonderful little pigs who never get enough. He pushed his ass back at my charging prick as if he could get it farther in. He clenched his muscle until it felt like he was fucking me and he kept begging me to do it harder.

I was surprised at how long I lasted, considering I'd been primed since I first saw him. I rode him full out, our juicy slap echoing through the garage, and when a climax beckoned, I made it known. A roar escaped me as everything tensed and when the pulse began I unleashed not only streams of cum but what seemed like every ounce of energy I'd ever possessed. Talk about getting off.

"Holy shit," my little friend said when I was finally spent. My cock slid out of him and I savored the gape of his pucker, red rim heated and wet.

When we'd mopped up and dressed I introduced myself.

"Rick, in town from San Francisco on business."

"I'm Tommy and I am very happy to know you."

He then led me into an elegant beachfront house that he told me belonged to his partner. "It's an open relationship," he assured me as we swigged ice water. "Jarrell is fucking his way across Italy at the moment," he added. "Our commitment is purely emotional."

"Must be nice. I've never managed that kind of thing."

"Keeps everyone happy all the way around."

When he asked if I wanted to shower, I told him no.

"Don't you either. I've been cleaned up all week. What I want now is dirty."

"Fine with me."

"You know what would be totally cool?" I asked. "A ride on that bike of yours. I've never done that and it's so opposite my life."

"You've never been on a bike? Wow, we have to take a ride and I know just the place. Topanga Canyon. It's up the coast into the Santa Monica Mountains."

"Sounds perfect, but I don't have any jeans with me."

He grinned.

"No problem. You're about Jarrell's size. Let's get you outfitted."

I was indeed Jarrell's size. His jeans, T-shirt and light jacket fit perfectly, as did a pair of boots.

"Does he ride with you?"

Tommy laughed.

"Not even. He was pissed I bought the bike, gets all huffy when I go for a ride, but he does get hot at the idea so I always return to a stiff dick and major fucking."

I started to flush at the idea, realizing it was me all over.

"The bike's a turn-on," I offered. "I saw you on it and got totally hard. God knows what riding it will do."

"Let's find out."

In the garage he handed me a helmet.

"I got it for Jarrell before I knew I'd be riding solo." He opened the garage door and gave me the basics of riding as a passenger. "Hold on to me, not the bike, so if the worst happens you'll be with me not it. Don't try to guide anything, just relax and go with the flow. I'll do the work, okay?"

I nodded, excitement building. As hot as I was for him, the motorcycle had almost as much appeal. He turned it around, rolled it outside and I followed. When the garage door closed he said to get on.

Swinging my leg over the thing, I had an odd cowboy sensation, like I was climbing onto a horse. Settling onto the long seat I asked him why he'd gotten this kind of motorcycle and not one of the popular garish kind.

"A crotch rocket? No thanks. This is a Triumph Bonneville, new but still with classic lines. This is what motorcycles really are. My dad had one when I was a kid and he'd take me for rides. He still has it, a '75 Triumph. Now hang on."

He hit the starter and the engine rumbled to life, surprising me at how much I could feel it. A few twists of the throttle, then a click of his foot and we rolled down the alley. As we turned up Thirteenth Street, climbing through Manhattan Beach toward Pacific Coast Highway, I marveled at the wind in my face and the feel of the motorcycle as we rounded corners and zoomed from stoplights. I did as Tommy instructed, relaxing, with him doing the work, which allowed an easy sort of sway through the turns. At one stoplight he reached back and squeezed my leg.

"You doing okay?"

"You bet."

Soon we were headed north on Pacific Coast Highway and it occurred to me how little adventure I had anymore, or maybe I never had. I was not an adventurous type for the most part. I worked hard, saw friends, but did little out of the ordinary and now here I was skipping out on work to ride up the coast with a sweet little hottie.

We sped through a string of beach towns: Marina Del Rey, Venice and Santa Monica. After that things spread out, the ocean always off to the left, beach by the mile, and to the right rolling hills punctuated now and then with a rocky outcropping. It was warm out but the bike made it cool, and I sucked in air like I'd never known it fresh before. The helmet I wore wasn't one of those Darth Vader full-face types, it was old-fashioned like the bike, open in front which allowed all of nature to hit me full force. The wind brought ocean smell mixed with nature's combination plate of greens and earth. I loved it.

The highway was straight for the most part but when we encountered the occasional curve I thrilled to the lean and sway, the engine pounding below, sending its low roar up through me. I'd straddled many a man but this was something else, my legs around pure power, and I began to understand the appeal of riding. Tommy was lucky to be up front right over the engine and have the big beast in his control. Fixing on this I couldn't help but become aroused, and as I gripped his waist I allowed one hand to slide down to his crotch. He squirmed on the seat as if welcoming the attention.

"We have to fuck!" I yelled over his shoulder and he nodded. Conversation was nearly impossible with the wind we created. I kept prodding him, squirming on the seat as my dick stiffened.

Suddenly an intersection was upon us and without hesitation, Tommy hung a quick right onto a two-lane road that climbed up away from the ocean and became one curve after another.

"Topanga Canyon," he called over his shoulder.

I soon saw the appeal. The road was total switchback as it rose higher and higher away from the coast. Native California scrub dotted the hills and as we got higher, trees filled in, pines and oaks mostly. The ocean smell faded as the heavy scent of pine took over.

Occasionally a cabin or rustic house perched near the road, but for the most part it seemed devoid of population. Tommy rode like he knew it well, and when we'd climbed so far I couldn't see the ocean anymore, he slowed and turned onto what looked like no more than a dirt path, and we bumped along until we were well into a compact grove of trees. Here he stopped and shut off the engine.

Before he could get off the bike, I got his zipper down and he eased up enough for me to free his dick. He was as hard as I was, and wet. I rubbed his precum around his knob, then pulled at him.

"I want to fuck on the bike," I said and he laughed. "I'm serious," I added.

I let go of him and took off my helmet, then climbed off the bike.

"Get your pants off," I said, "but leave the rest."

He did as told while I ditched my jeans and shorts but kept on the boots since the ground was a mess of pine needles, rocks and dirt. I tossed my jacket and T-shirt so I was naked save for the boots while Tommy wore only his tee, jacket and boots. I got a condom from my pocket while Tommy secured the bike on its center stand after finding a solid spot. I then climbed on.

Tommy stood working his cock while I suited up and once sheathed and lubed with spit, I invited him aboard. "Facing front, like you're still riding," I said and he did as asked, balancing on the pegs, butt in the air as he leaned forward while clutching the handlebars.

What a sight. I took him at the hips and eased him down onto my throbbing pole while I leaned back just a tad to maintain maximum leverage.

"Hah!" I said. "It's totally possible."

Much as I wanted to take him, I went slow because this had to be the ultimate. I looked up at the trees surrounding us, daylight filtering through the branches, and I sucked in more of that pine-scented air as I began an easy undulating thrust. Tommy proved to be an expert rider, working his ass in sync with me until we had a sweet rhythm going. It set the bike rocking on its stand while I enjoyed the most singular fuck of my life. Tommy, meanwhile, started frantically jerking his cock and let out a "Shit yeah!" as he sprayed cum onto the gas tank. I leaned forward and watched over his shoulder, noting he carried a good load, the sight of which got me so worked up I lost my easy rhythm and began to fuck him full out, slamming my dick into him with hard thrusts that brought me up off the seat. The bike shuddered beneath us and a fleeting concern passed through my mind about it maybe falling over but I didn't care, I was lost to a major bike fuck and was going to come like never before. And then it hit and I let out a howl, digging into Tommy's hips as I pumped out enough jizz to drown him. He held on to the handlebars as I rammed it home and kept ramming, even when I was empty because it was the best ever, and holy Christ I didn't want to quit.

Finally I went soft and slumped back. Tommy slid off of me

and collapsed forward over the gas tank, arms draped on the handlebars.

"Jarrell doesn't know what he's missing," I said between gasps, which set Tommy laughing.

When he managed to speak all he said was, "Jarrell who?"

"I guess we should get off this thing," I finally said and we climbed from the bike. My resourceful little friend then pulled up the seat and extracted a small towel and a bottle of water.

"All this and a Boy Scout too," I said.

"Ever prepared."

We shared the water and cleaned up but didn't want to leave.

"Let's make a bed," Tommy said and he began laying out our clothes until there was cover enough for two. Not the most comfortable spot but enough to stretch out beside him and enjoy the green canopy.

"I've never done this," I confessed.

"What, sex on a bike or sex in the woods?"

"Either. I'm a total businessman, always striving, always in meetings. Even my dates are like that, my boyfriends are always success stories when what I need, I now see, is a little biker boy." Here I reached over to squeeze his thigh. "This has been the most liberating experience of my life."

"Me too," Tommy said, rolling onto his side to face me. He slid a hand over my chest, played with a nipple. "I've never had sex on the bike."

"Tell me that's not a cum rag you had packed with the water."

He laughed.

"No, it's for emergencies, the water too. The towel usually mops up brake fluid or something."

"So we've liberated each other," I concluded.

He leaned in and kissed me, then snuggled up and soon we began to doze. It felt wonderful to let everything slip away,

Tommy's soft snore mingling with sweet summer air, bird chatter and pure calm. I looked at patches of sky until they faded.

When I woke it was to Tommy's mouth on my dick. He was down between my legs sucking expertly and I opened to him, let his hand cup my balls. As I swam in the feel of his attentions, I noted our little grotto had lost most of its light. Dusk was upon us but I didn't care. My cock was stirring and that trumps all concern.

As Tommy fed, I pulled at his arm and he got the idea. He reversed position to climb over me and drop his cock into my mouth and there we lay, sucking dick in the great outdoors but I wasn't satisfied with just his cock so I traded hand for mouth, milking him steadily while my lips sought what I really wanted, his bunghole. Driving my tongue into his crack, I found his nasty little center and pushed in. He squeezed his sphincter in welcome.

We kept working each other until the juice started to rise, so I backed off because I wanted to fuck him again. Much as I'd have liked to come in that sweet mouth, I wanted one more on the bike. And I told him.

We untangled and stood, each with hand on cock, and I realized I didn't necessarily want it on the bike but I wanted the motorcycle to be part of it, my own demented brand of threesome. I pulled on a condom and told Tommy to stand beside the motorcycle and lean over the seat. He grinned at the idea, then did as told and I approached, pulled apart his pink cheeks to get at his center.

"Fuck, yeah," I said as I pushed in.

He spread his arms so one lay across the gas tank, the other draped along the seat and back fender, which heightened the scene for me. I looked down at my dick going up his ass and farther, to the engine down to my left, recalling how it had sent its rumbles up through me and got me hard. No wonder so many guys rode bikes. They all had stiff dicks.

Darkness began to overtake us as we enjoyed our final bike fuck. It wasn't a quick one, being third of the day, and that in itself seemed remarkable as I usually couldn't do more than one or two, and usually one of those was by my own hand. But something about the motorcycle and its rider combined, something wild and earthy and free stirred my very core and kept my prong hard as a stallion's.

When the rise began I didn't hold back. It was the end of a perfect day and what better way than to unload my very last drop.

"I'm gonna…" was all I managed before I let go but this time I didn't slam into Tommy or set the bike rocking. This time I just kept a steady thrust and allowed the climax to engulf the whole of me, sending pulses from cock and balls to spine to calves to toes and back, to take my breath away, make my heart pound. There in the woods I was reduced to pure animal. If I'd had claws Tommy would have been scraped raw.

In total darkness, I withdrew and tossed the rubber. Tommy righted himself and pressed against me.

"You are amazing," he said. "You can't get away from me. I won't let you."

"Don't worry," I assured him. "I'm not about to." With that we kissed briefly, then attended to practical matters. The temperature was dropping rapidly. Tommy put on the motorcycle's big headlight so we could see what we were doing and we hurriedly dressed. Donning our helmets, we climbed onto the bike and carefully made our way from our little grove back onto the path and finally the road. From there we descended to the coastal highway and zoomed back to Manhattan Beach.

I almost dreaded returning to the big house on Thirteenth

Street because it was reality, some other life that belonged to a guy named Jarrell. In the garage as Tommy pulled the bike onto its stand, I felt an ache that almost took my breath away. I had no idea what was next.

"C'mon in," Tommy said and I followed him inside.

"Guess I'd better change back into my own clothes," I told him.

"Why?" he asked.

"Well, I have a job to get back to and you've got a partner and—"

"Jarrell isn't due back for three more weeks so unless you really have to get back to that job, you're welcome to stay."

Until that moment I hadn't considered our day together anything more than a two-wheeled one-nighter.

"Really?" I said because the offer seemed too good to be true.

"Really." He hugged me to him. "You're the best thing that's ever happened to me and I'd like to explore that."

"Me too."

"So can you call in sick or something?"

I thought of the forty-two sick days I'd accumulated. Known in the office for never calling in sick much less taking vacations, all I had to do was invent something plausible.

"Yes, I can. Something serious, maybe pneumonia. I'll call, say I've been at the emergency room all day."

Once I'd hatched the plot, it all came together and I was surprised at how easily I changed from businessman to runaway biker. As Tommy and I settled into bed that night, I told him I wanted another ride the next day.

"Sure. Where do you want to go?"

Rolling onto him, grinding my crotch against his, I told him, "Why do we have to go anywhere?"

# READY

## Xan West

Daddy said I was ready for this. I trusted him, and yet…I didn't feel ready. I wasn't sure I'd ever feel ready. But I showed up anyway, knowing that part of what would get me through it was obedience, choosing to give myself to his will.

Some scenes change you. Sometimes you don't know they will until they have. Sometimes you can tell beforehand. I knew I would walk out changed that night, if I could just get through it. I could taste self-doubt in the back of my throat as I approached the garage. Could I do this, for real?

I was dressed as he told me to be, in my father's old clothes: a worn pair of boots that used to be his, which I had painstakingly restored; his old jeans; the belt that he had left hanging on the wall; and his old Harley T-shirt, faded and worn until it was a soft whisper of comfort on my skin. When my father left us, I pulled his belt off the wall, grabbed his old boots that he had left in the back of the closet and went searching through the laundry for his clothes. I can still hear the sound of his Harley driving away, still see his long hair streaming behind him. I slept holding his clothes for six months; when I turned thirteen I hid them away until I was old enough to wear them.

I wore only my father's clothes that night, because that was what Daddy asked me to do. I tried to stand tall and stop trembling as I stood in front of him in them. Daddy walked slowly around me, and the sound of his uneven gait on the concrete calmed me in its familiarity. His hand snaked out and unbuckled my belt, whipping it from my jeans, and he wrapped it around my wrists and forearms, securing me. I began to breathe, slow and even, my father's belt wrapped around me. Daddy knew exactly how to calm me and how to scare me; he made a delicious dance of it, and that dance was just beginning.

Daddy shoved me onto a chair and attached the belt to it. There is nothing that feels safer to me than bondage. Even if the rest is scary, if I concentrate on the sensation of being bound, I can make my way through it.

Daddy was looming over me, his T-shirt riding up, his large brown belly brushing against my head. He smelled so good, a musky sweaty scent mixed with oil and metal. That smell alone gets my dick hard, the smell that tells me a man has been working hard on a bike. It was clear he had; he was dirty as only a mechanic can get dirty, and I ached to suck the grease off his thick fingers.

Sometimes I think about Daddy and get so giddy knowing that I get to be his boy, that a scrawny faggot like me is lucky enough to be claimed by this big tough bear of a man. This was one of those times, as he rested a paw on my head and pressed my mouth against his stomach. Daddy was big enough to keep me safe, strong enough to hold all of me, cruel enough to give me exactly what I needed, and scary enough to keep me coming back for more.

At the moment when I relaxed into feeling safe, I heard it: that unmistakable buzzing noise that only clippers produce. I swallowed, lifted my eyes to his, and began begging.

"Please, Daddy. No, please don't do this. I can't take it, Daddy."

I began to shake my head, frantic, until his grip tightened in my hair. I stared up at him, whimpering softly.

"You have to let go, boy. It's time. You are carrying so much in your hair, boy. I know it's hard; you've been growing it since your father left. But it's time to let go of it. Ten years is long enough."

"I don't think I can do it, Daddy."

"You are ready, boy. And I'm right here with you. Daddy's right here. He's not going anywhere. You can do this."

I took a deep breath, staring into his eyes. They were resolute. He was not going to let me get out of this without safewording.

"Yes, Sir," I whispered.

The buzzing against my head was all I could hear as my hair began to fall. His hand was gripped in my hair tightly, holding me still, the clippers moving firmly across my scalp as tears rolled down my face. I could feel his dick pressed against my neck, and then he moved around me, resting his knee on my cock as he pressed into me, shaving the front of my head. I sobbed into his belly, gripping him tightly, overwhelmed. It seemed like it was excruciatingly slow, and I closed my eyes tight, willing myself to breathe through it, trembling. Finally it stopped. Daddy ran his hand along my head and groaned.

"You feel so good, boy."

He pulled out his dick and began rubbing it all over my head, growling.

"Damn, boy, you sure do get me hard. Just feeling that stubble against my dick makes me want to shoot."

Then Daddy rubbed his cock against my cheeks, soaking in my tears.

"That's my good boy. Get my dick wet with your tears."

He moved behind me and forced my head down, covering my mouth and nose with his greasy hand, taking my breath, as he thrust his dick along my head, groaning. My heart started racing. My head was filled with the scent of motor oil. I was trembling, desperate to please Daddy, struggling to breathe. He growled as he came, his cum drooling onto my face, covering my head, and then he released my breath.

"Thank you, Daddy," escaped my lips within seconds. It felt so right to say it.

There was a click by my ear, and I went still. I knew that noise. It was Daddy's knife. It touched my lips, and they pursed to kiss the blade. Then I felt cold steel against my throat. My eyes were blurry, my head full of fog, and I was frozen.

"Time to let go, boy."

That only meant one thing. He was going to cut off my clothes.

All of me shouted no at once. He wasn't really going to do that, for real, was he? But he did, even as I said no, over and over, he growled yes, slicing the shirt off me. When it was done, he moved to the front to go after the jeans.

"How can you do this, Daddy? How can you be so mean to me?" I yelled into his face.

He pulled the shirt from my skin and stuffed it into my mouth.

"Scream all you want, boy. Scream as loud and as much as you want. Call me every name you can. I'm still going to be here."

I did, at the top of my lungs, screaming around the shirt, my mouth working to expel it, until I spit it in his face, cursing and yelling that he was a Bad Daddy, that I hated him, how could he do this to me. It eventually devolved into screaming repeatedly, "Why are you doing this to me, Daddy?" until I began to sob, my lungs struggling, my legs bare, the jeans gone in pieces, left naked except for the boots. He gathered me into him, unbinding me from the chair, holding me against his chest, letting me sob it out.

"Such a brave good boy," he whispered, murmuring repeatedly, "Daddy's here," until the mantra finally registered, and I attuned to it, my breathing following its rhythm. Daddy is home, and safety, and love. He is cruel and scary, and demanding too, but that feels just like home, and somehow is part of how I know he loves me. In some corner of my mind I hold on to the fact that I asked him to do this to me, but part of his magic is that I do truly feel helpless to stop him, certain that he runs this small bit of universe that is ours, free to hate him and to please him because I know that he is in it for the long haul. He makes sure to remind me when we go deep, like we did that night, but I know it's true. I belong to Daddy, and he is here to stay.

He pulled me to my feet, pulled a lever, and I watched it lower from the ceiling, amazed. I knew just what it was. You see, Daddy doesn't ride anymore, not since his leg got fucked up in that last crash. He still works on bikes, builds them, repairs them, but Daddy doesn't ride anymore. His last bike, a sweet '40s-style Harley he built himself, was never the same after that crash. Neither was Daddy. So he worked the bike into something else entirely, which he kept chained to the ceiling in his shop.

He had taken that bike he built and turned it into a sling. But not just any sling: one you lie in facedown. It spreads your legs, gives you a seat to support yourself, and is built for four-point bondage. It has a chrome face piece that gives a perfect view of the shop below. I had never been in it, but I knew it was there, had watched him build it. It was his secret fantasy to imagine me riding it, floating above him, watching him work on bikes. He promised me that I would be the first to ride it, and he had been waiting for me to be ready. He thought it was time.

I stared at it and decided I must be crazy. How the hell could I even consider doing this? Only a crazy person would face his fear of falling in this way. What was I thinking? My heart started racing. I could feel tension in my feet and calves as running seemed like the perfect choice, the only choice. Who cared if I was naked, my arms tied behind my back with my father's belt? I had boots on; I could run fast in those. I tasted fear like metal in my mouth. How could he ask this of me? He knew why I didn't do this kind of stuff, knew what it meant that I had even considered it. He loved me, how could he ask me to do this for him? Did he actually believe I could do it?

Daddy stood behind me, his arms wrapped around me, hands clasped in the center of my chest, feeling the energy surge and build. I could hear his calm breathing, feel his breath on my neck, his chest rise and fall against my back.

"I know you are afraid, boy. This is what courage is about. You can do this. Let me show you what it is to ride your fear. That's what it's like to be on a bike, feeling it move with you, part of you, no barriers between you and danger, all that power and courage under you, in you. Do this for me, boy. Let me teach you why I love this bike, even with all it took from me. Please, boy. Let me share this with you."

I couldn't breathe. Tears rolled down my cheeks, and I leaned back into him. He rarely talked about this loss, and had never said please to me before. He wanted me to give him everything, and in that moment I was so full of love for him, so sure he saw me, so secure in his arms, that I thought I might actually be able to do it, for real.

"Yes, Daddy," I said, my voice hoarse.

He let go of me, untied my arms, and attached cuffs to my wrists and ankles. It felt so good to feel the leather holding me, so safe. Then he moved toward the bike-sling, holding it still. I just had to get on. Okay, I could do that. Maybe. I tried some slow breathing, but my heart would not stop racing. I walked up to it, and got on my knees in it, wiggling forward until my arms were in the right spot, my face settled. It was cold, chrome against my cheeks and chest, my cock pressed into the leather seat. He attached the cuffs, and then let it go. All I could see was the floor, as the bike-sling began to sway.

"No," I shrieked.

"You can do this, boy. I know you can. Breathe. And concentrate on the pain. It will help."

Then he hit me with something that felt like fire. I knew that sensation. Daddy had made a flail. The handle was the brake rod from that very same motorcycle. The tails were made from rim strips, rubber and evil. Daddy had made this tool as a way to honor his last ride, and the flail knew it, held all of that rage and pain and mourning in it. It was a path from him to me that fed me all of that, so that I could transmute it. That was my gift to Daddy, to take his pain and rage and sorrow, and transform it, and he was right. It did help. All I could think about was taking it. Not the way the blows rocked the sling, not the fact that I could fall. Just the fire eating into my skin, opening me, moving through me. I was nothing but a receptacle for Daddy, taking everything he needed to give me, flying on that, knowing I was useful to him, that I belonged to him. I knew how to do this, I had a lot of practice, and that familiarity was what kept me from fighting to get free. When it stopped, I held my breath, smelling alcohol, feeling it cool on my skin. I was bleeding, and it felt right that I would be. I could feel the blood seeping down and it was perfect.

"Now you can ride, boy."

I was rising, higher, blinking my eyes open and watching Daddy get farther away. He moved out of my line of vision and I screamed, suddenly very aware of exactly where I was. Way too high up.

"I'm going to work on this engine, boy. When you hear it purr, that's when you get to come down."

He began to work, then, as if I had nothing to say about this. He was right. I didn't. I was stuck up there, without him. Alone with my fear. Fuck. Was I ready for this? I began to breathe faster, until the movement of my body awoke the pain, and it centered me again. Okay. I could do this for Daddy. Or at least I could try.

I was so high up, it was hard to look. I could feel myself swinging with the bike-sling and gripped hard with my thighs, my heart in my throat. Then I was back there.

They taunted me as they did it, held me over the edge calling me sissy and faggot, my body a bruise from what they had already done to it. They egged each other on, fear hinting in their voices, as I begged them to stop, to let me down. At fifteen my queerness seemed branded on my skin for them to see, and that was why I was here. Roger had started it, scared someone would find out that he let me suck his cock in the bathroom after the previous night's game. I was used to the bullying, used to the taunts and isolation. But this was the first time I thought that I might not make it out alive. They were laughing as they pulled me back to the edge, egging each other on as they stripped me naked and tossed my clothes off the roof, holding me down, my torso hanging over the edge of the roof, gravel digging into my knees. They spread my legs, and I begged them to stop, but they wouldn't, they couldn't stop now. It was cold, the concrete edge of the roof. My head swam, dizzy with the possibility of falling, unbalanced, sure if they let me go I would fall and die, just wanting to survive. They called me faggot, over and over, as they hurt me and rammed themselves into me and I begged them to let me live. They left me there on that roof, naked, bleeding, with a tribute of spit and spunk on my skin.

I lay there trapped, facing the same sensation coupled with memory, naked, legs spread, fearing I would fall, spunk and blood on my skin, just like it was. The memory circled around and around, until I started noticing what was different now. I felt the smooth chrome against my face, looked down to find Daddy working on that engine, felt the leather against my wrists holding me safe. The sounds were different, their hands were not on me. I was alone. The words reached through that dark tunnel and found me, wrapped around me like bandages. *I choose this.*

I choose this man for my Daddy. I choose to face my fear. I choose to live. I choose to be a faggot. I choose this. Those boys may have tried to shame me for who I am, but Daddy loves me for it, wants me because of it. Daddy sees strength and courage in me for all I have survived and all I can do, where they only saw weakness. I choose this life, this fear, this rage. I make it mine. I may feel like my stomach is in my throat, but I'm still here, still facing it. I am no longer in high school, no longer hiding from my desire, no longer ashamed of who I am—I live my life every day as an out queer, and I'm not alone in that like I used to be. I would choose this any day over the closeted misery that Roger is probably living. I choose to be a faggot.

I looked down at Daddy, and I felt so close to him. He trusted me enough to show me his need, saw into me, found courage I didn't think I had, and brought it out to show it to me. He asked me to ride the motorcycle that transformed his life and created a way for it to transform mine.

Daddy revved that engine down below, and I could feel my

dick begin to swell. Then he looked up at me and held my eyes with his as he revved the engine again. I squirmed. Daddy put the engine aside and picked up the belt, my father's belt. He folded it over and snapped it. I could feel my eyes widen as my dick jumped at the sound. Daddy began to lower me toward him, the promise of pain in his eyes.

I came to rest level with his cock. The leather drove into me, and I screamed; it was such an intense way to break that isolation. Daddy moved around to slide between my legs, his cock pressing against me, and began to beat me for real. He beat me with that belt as if he were possessed, ravenous, wanting my blood to splatter, aching to rip me open. There was intense violence in the air; it crackled with feral energy. I wanted this, so bad. Wanted to bleed all over that belt tonight, mark it with my pride and transformation, claim it as mine.

"Tell me," he said.

The words caught in my throat. He snarled, the belt slicing into my back.

"I'm your faggot, Daddy," I said hoarsely.

"Keep saying it, boy. After every stroke."

It was so hard to get the words out. So hard to breathe. Daddy growled as he beat me, and I said it, louder as it went on, until it started feeling right in my mouth. I was his faggot, and proud to be, and saying it repeatedly had reminded me of that, made it solid. I could feel the energy building as I said it, as if my words were filling the room, ready to explode it at any second. He lay the belt along my back, pulled out his cock, slid on a condom, and lubed it up.

"Tell me that you want it, boy."

"Please fuck me, Daddy. I want you inside me, want your cock so bad. Please fuck your faggot, Daddy."

"Lick that chrome for me, boy."

I began to lick it. It was cold and tangy. Tears rolled down my face until I was tasting them along with the chrome, the salty metal taste of fear and desire rolled together. Would he leave me aching like this forever? He began to beat me again, and I shuddered, licking chrome for all I was worth, whimpering.

"That's my good boy. I know it tastes so good. Lick Daddy's bike right."

He lay the belt down on my back again and slid into me, all slow like he wanted to savor it. Then he picked up the belt, his cock deep in my ass, still, claiming me. The belt drove into me again, pain making me contract around his cock.

"I'm your faggot, Daddy," I said into the chrome, then kept on licking, as he pulled back and began to ram me with his cock.

"That's my good boy. Keep telling me. Don't stop saying it."

It was hard to focus, his cock felt so good, but I needed to do what Daddy said, so I tried to concentrate on saying the words.

"Such a good hole for Daddy. Such a good faggot hole. That's what you are. Daddy's hole to fuck. You love getting your ass fucked, don't you, faggot? It's exactly what the boy needs, so he can't forget who he is. My faggot. My hole. That's it, boy, grab on to my cock, work it, faggot."

I kept saying it over and over for Daddy, wanting to be good, losing track of everything except the words in my mouth and the words in my ear and his dick in my ass. He began to rock the bike-sling, slamming me onto his cock.

I screamed the words for him: "I'm your faggot, Daddy!"

"Yes you are, boy. That's it. Ride Daddy's cock. Such a good faggot. I need you, boy. Need to fuck you, and scare you, and claim you. Give it to me."

I screamed the words at him, heart racing as I felt like I was falling onto his cock, so angry that he would do this, screamed my rage through those words, my cock aching.

"Daddy!" I sobbed. "I'm your faggot, Daddy, I'm your faggot."
He jacked me onto him, growling.

"Yes, boy, you are my faggot hole to fuck, and you feel so
damn good. Come for me, boy. Let me feel you come around my
cock. Don't forget to say the words as you do it."

"I am your faggot, Daddy," I groaned, my cock bursting,
sobbing.

I kept murmuring the words, as he rammed my hole onto his
dick. I was floating, flying, just his faggot hole, and so glad to
belong to him, to be used by him. Wanting to help him come,
aching to feel him spurting into me, wishing he wasn't wearing
a condom, wishing I could feel his cum deep inside me, ingest it,
take it into me.

"Please, Daddy. Please come in my ass. I'm your faggot hole,
Daddy. Please fill your faggot hole."

Daddy growled, grabbing the sling and moving it quickly,
slamming me onto his cock. I screamed, sobbing, begging him
to come, wanting his cum so bad, fear tasting like chrome in my
mouth. He snarled as he rammed my faggot hole onto his dick. I
shuddered, so glad to feel his cream spurting, taking it in.

"That's my good faggot," he said.

He released the bondage and brought me down slowly,
holding me, rubbing my freshly shaven head, licking the tears
from my cheeks. I felt lighter, like I was filled with bubbles, and
yet more solid, taller. I met his eyes.

"Thank you, Daddy."

"You are most welcome, boy. I'm glad we waited until you
were ready. It was worth it, don't you think?"

"Oh, yes, Daddy."

I fell asleep that night in his arms, his naked chest against my
back, his T-shirt cuddled in my arms.

# ROAD RIDER

## Jay Starre

Dason Flexhaug was a road rider.

Eyes darting to the side of the empty Egyptian highway to take in the emerald sheen of grass and young trees vanquishing sand and rock, he could hardly believe it had been only a decade since the Collapse.

Things were pretty much settling down around the world. Pretty much. He'd only been fifteen when the shit hit the fan, and all things considered he was one of the lucky ones. He was still alive.

He lay almost prone on the back of his Xchange560, his booted feet behind and stretched back onto the heavy foot pads. The bike was brand new, replaced on his last trip to Detroit in New Canada where the Chrysler-BMW Conglomerate churned out the latest vehicles for the drastically dwindled masses of the global market.

His helmet, the latest style in chrome green to match the shimmering emerald of his bike, cradled his head in contoured perfection like a second scalp—and his personal addition to that helmet, the swooping wings on either side, flattened out to offer the least wind resistance.

His arms stretched down to grip the low handlebars with hands encased in opal green leather, shot through with veins of pink and blue, catching the late afternoon rays of the sun like rippling water in a cataract.

Otherwise, he was butt naked.

He grinned broadly, showing his straight white teeth between full lips. He had a great smile—and used it. You never knew who you'd run into in his line of work. It paid to be friendly. He had a great body too, and he often used it as casually as his smile.

He was heading south and already far from a bustling Cairo, the capital of the Union of North Africa, and still one of the largest cities on Earth with a population of nearly one million. He ate up the distance at a steady 120 klicks, his bike vibrating under his naked body pleasantly. A solar-powered electric engine, it didn't roar and throb like bikes of the past. But the steady thrum of tires against roadway offered its own seductive rhythm.

The wind whistled around his ears with the keening moan of freedom, then swam over his widespread shoulders and down his spine in a sensual thrust of pressure to dive directly into his parted asscrack. Air spiraled over his bared asshole, tickling and teasing.

Sprawled facedown as he was, thighs and arms cradling the humming machine beneath, wind caressing his naked body, and asshole constantly licked and sucked on by nature's warm breath, it was no wonder his cock jerked stiff under his belly. The leather seat was smooth and supple under him. A sheen of sweat lubricated his belly and crotch. His cock pulsed in it, oozing precum in a constant dribble.

It was a perfect day.

The Nile flowed turgidly below to his right, a flattened sheen of azure. Palms and other trees hugged the shore, while the hardy new grasses that were settling over the vast desert sands on all sides vied with golden dunes and orange rock. Wildlife, antelope and wild camels for the most part, appeared at intervals to populate a landscape abandoned by humans.

He couldn't stop grinning—and his cock couldn't stop drooling. With his asshole constantly sucked and kissed by the wind, he was tempted more than once to pull over and satisfy it with a big dildo, but the expectation of his rendezvous in the morning proved enough to forestall that.

The sun was a fat red ball in the west when he approached his destination for the night.

Slowing down drastically, he engaged the handlebar-motionary. With gliding ease, the handlebars rose up, his arms along with them. At the same time, his footpads rotated, sliding forward as the handlebars came up.

In a moment he was seated upright, his booted feet now in front and ahead, his arms still widespread but now above the sleek body of the machine. He settled in, leaning slightly back, the reduced wind now sliding over him in an upward curve to roll over his bare shoulders.

This was the position boot used for always sprints Heat up he gazed around as he turned off the main roadway onto the secondary highway that led to his destination. The bike throbbed under him quietly, his fat balls nestled in the slippery leather seat, his asshole now pouting as it pressed against it. His cock reared up in front of him, curved like a sword to bounce against his rippled belly.

The wind now massaged his cock instead of his asshole. His thighs clenched around the sides of the bike, his asshole kissed the seat. He leaned back and sighed.

A few delicious minutes of warm wind massaging his plump

balls and bobbing hard-on had him pleasantly aching all over. The drool of precum dried on his flared cockhead, while sweat pooled around his balls and asscrack. Sublime! It was as if feathery fingers stroked his cock all over, from base to crown, constant and insistent. He could almost come...if he wanted to. But not yet. The best awaited on the morrow.

The setting sun bathed the two temples ahead in an umber glow: Abu Simbel.

He parked in front of the temple of Ramses II. On his right stood the Pharaoh's tribute to his Queen Nefertiti.

He straddled the bike and gazed on the ancient wonder as he flicked on his speaker and made his report. "This is Dason Flex-haug reporting live from Abu Simbel in the Egyptian Preserve. What can I tell you about the ancient people who built these monuments? Not much, and most of you don't give a fuck anyway. Yesterday is gone, today and tomorrow are what matters. You've seen the desert coming to life all around me as I drove south. That's what I'm here to report about."

His single headlight, a curved oval of sleek symmetry, served a second purpose. It was a camera and recorded the image he himself gazed up at. It had been recording his entire journey and broadcasting it live to monitors all over the world. The masses loved his travel show!

He was called the Road Rider, but also the Road Writer. It was the best job in the world, he figured, although his sideline, tour guide, was pretty damn fine too.

When he'd completed his spiel, he set up camp. Out of the compartment under his seat, he produced the essentials: torch for starting his campfire, compact pistol for bagging a desert hare for his supper, cooking and eating utensils. A grove of orange trees offered a twin bonus of fruit and a sheltered spot for his camp.

A rabbit shot, skinned and roasted over the fire, three tasty desert oranges for dessert, and a vitamin bar from his stash were all he needed. He leaned back on his bike and settled in for a cozy sleep, footpads up, leather seat extended behind to create a headrest. Naked still, but for his shimmering emerald boots and matching gloves, he stared up at implacable stars, unchanged regardless of the cataclysms that had befallen the human race in the early twenty-first century.

In the morning he waited. Straddling his Xchange, he posed provocatively for his expected rendezvous. Out of the north it approached, the massive cargo helicopter ferrying his client.

The fat flying beast was painted bright yellow and impossible to miss as it drew closer. Across its side splashed the words SYDNEY SALVAGE. The Australian mega-company was now the largest in the world, in a time when salvaging the detritus of five billion dead and their possessions was the biggest business around.

Australia had been one of the lucky countries. An island continent, it was the only place on Earth that had escaped the flu pandemic that killed off two-thirds of humanity. And double-blessed, it was one place where the climate actually had improved, along with Canada, Scandinavia and Russia.

His client owned Sydney Salvage. He was now the richest man on Earth.

Dason waved, posing in a prominent location just before the imposing statue of Ramses II. The helicopter landed in a whir of dust that tickled his bare flesh in a spray of fine prickles. He didn't mind. In fact, the sandy blast only stiffened his curved hard-on.

Billy Macleod emerged. The helicopter rose immediately and sped off. They were left alone.

Fair-haired and slender, Billy approached. Dason waited, straddling his bike, hard-on in plain sight. He was well aware of the image he projected, broad chest tanned and smooth, arms long and muscular, thighs powerful as they hugged the sides of his bike, boots, gloves and helmet shimmering emerald to match his machine in the morning sunlight.

Cock stiff and dripping.

Billy Macleod wore only a pair of sturdy shorts and a light T-shirt, small packsack strung across one shoulder. Good. He'd obeyed his instructions. Bring little or nothing.

"Three things off the bat, Macleod," Dason instructed, his glowing grin softening the clipped demands that followed. "First, we take only what fits in the seat compartment and you leave the rest here in the desert. Second, you strip off. We travel in the buff. Third, do you want to be the biker bitch first, or you want me in that role?"

To his credit, the blond Aussie laughed pleasantly, and immediately began to strip, pale blue eyes roaming over Dason's powerful body and upthrust hard-on.

He'd brought a helmet as required and naturally it was the best money could buy. Butter yellow and emblazoned with the SYDNEY SALVAGE logo, it slid over his mop of blond hair and contracted to fit snugly. As the other man discarded T-shirt and shorts and finally expensive silk underwear, Dason sat back and watched.

Slender, yes, but graced with supple muscle tone and smoothly healthy freckled flesh, he also boasted a surprisingly well-rounded bubble butt that jutted out from a slim waist in pale glory.

"Nice cock, Macleod. Looks like I'll enjoy being the bitch when it's my turn," Dason commented with a broadened grin as his wealthy client's dangling dick reared outward and upward to jerk up pink against his smooth belly.

Billy Macleod finally spoke. "I'll try out the biker bitch role first, mate. Shall we get on with it?"

Dason liked that. No fucking around. Just get to it. He
dismounted with a laugh and raised the shiny green leather seat
to stow the few belongings Macleod had brought that he deemed
worthy. The expensive packsack and other less worthy items he
discarded at the feet of Ramses II.

"No worries, mate, my helicopter will pick it up later. Now,
do I mount in front? Is that where a biker bitch sits?"

Dason was liking this dude more and more. He was quick.

"Yep. Get your ass up here between my legs. You're about to
take the ride of your life."

The blond's grin was bright as he obeyed, throwing one lean
leg over the bike in front of Dason, offering a brief glimpse of
a deep asscrack and a tightly puckered hole before settling in to
lean back against his host.

The rising sun was on their left, the azure Nile on their right
as they hit the road and headed south. The morning passed in
a sedate tease as Dason maintained their speed at a decorous
seventy klicks or so.

The wind was just strong enough to caress their bare flesh
rather than batter it, and with the upright saddle position in
place, his client enjoyed a comfortable seat with slim legs
forward, golden boots above Dason's on their own footpads,
and hands free to either grip Dason's extended forearms, or if he
wished, stroke his own lengthy boner.

The fleshy ass spread over the seat in front of him rested
against Dason's crotch. He allowed his own stiff rod to slide
up between the parted cheeks to rest there, pulsing and dripping as they motored along. Every now and then, he pumped it
along the crack seductively, reaffirming his position as boss, and
Macleod's as bitch.

Kilometers of Egyptian landscape fell behind. The spring
rains that had only recently subsided had left behind a redolent

stench of new growth. The river itself was becoming turgid and brown. The inundation approached.

Wildlife grew more common, especially down in the river and on its banks. Hippos cavorted in their slow dance, waterfowl rose and fell in waves, and nasty-looking crocs bathed in the sunlight. In the surrounding desert, herds of wild asses, goats and sheep began to appear alongside the antelope and camels.

Fascinating as that was, both men grew more and more enraptured by the play of cock in crack as sweat lathered under their butts and balls. Leaning back comfortably with extended arms on the bike's handlebars, Dason did little enough to encourage his client just yet. His gentle strokes and pumps of cock along that slippery-smooth asscrack grew more frequent, but otherwise he left Billy Macleod to his own devices.

The young businessman at first was content to lean back against the solid muscle behind, thighs splayed and ass teased by that stiff poker. His own cock bobbed up pink and proud, but at first he pretended to ignore it. At last, he couldn't stand it anymore. The constant caress of warm wind that swirled in a teasing vortex up between his legs, around his sweaty nuts and then in a column of stroking heat over his boner, grew more and more exciting.

He'd never done anything like this!

Finally, one gloved hand dropped to clasp the base of his slim but exceedingly long cock. Instantly his back arched and he groaned and thrust up with his hips, then countered by sliding back with his bare ass against the plump meat lodged in his buttcrack.

"Looks like you're finally ready to be the bitch," Dason yelled over the wind in the blond's ear.

"Fuck yeah, mate! Give me that biker cock!"

"Fine. But you have to give me that bitch hole, bud!"

That said, he engaged the footpad-motionary and Macleod's feet suddenly rose up enough so he could lift his butt off the bike to squat over the cock behind him. With a whoop of excitement the rich businessman wriggled his cute white butt around over the upthrust hard-on behind him and managed to plant his puckered asshole right on target.

Dason laughed along with him, leaning farther back and aiming. The blunt crown of his cock was more a battering ram than anything else, and it took a few moments of grunting and squirming for the blond to capture it with his snug anal ring and begin to swallow.

In a half-stand and squat, he bit his full lip and began to sit on that sweat-lubed poker. His ass and crack were well-lathered with sweat, but Dason took pity and added a great gob of spit to the straining juncture of cockhead and butthole. Laughing, he gobbed more spit onto his cock and watched as his blond client cried out against the whine of the wind and sucked in the entire knob.

Snug asslips encased the head of his cock in a slippery squeeze. Dason added his own cry of joy to Macleod's shouts.

"You're a tight fucker! Go on, ride it like a true biker bitch!"

Dason's shouted command galvanized the blond and as his dark eyes darted from highway to pale round butt, he watched Macleod gore himself on thick fuckpipe. Grunting and shouting, Macleod slowly sat, his distended asslips flushed bright pink against the freckled ivory of his smooth buttcrack.

He dropped down a few inches, his rounded ass jiggling with strain, rose up an inch, then dropped lower, swallowing more and more cock each time. Dason merely leaned back and let the little fucker ride it, increasing their speed just an increment at a time so that the wind grew stronger, and the landscape flew by more quickly.

The blond did an amazing job of stuffing his tight ass with that enormous pole. His sphincter strained and stretched in a throbbing squeeze as it engulfed more cock until finally, with a triumphant suck, it settled down over the base. He took cock to the balls.

Dason's breath was heaving by this time. The fucker's asshole was a clamping vise around his throbbing cock. The snug hole pulsed in a rapid squeeze and grasp that had his heart pounding. It was awesome!

"Time to fuck! Here we go," he shouted.

Engaging the motionary at its highest speed, he caused their positions to abruptly alter. They were thrown forward as the pair went from half supine to full prone in one breathtaking plunge. Footpads sped backward as handlebars dropped down and forward.

All at once, Dason was sprawled on top of his blond client— with cock buried deep in his pulsing asshole.

"Ride your bitch, mate!" Macleod whooped.

Dason snorted out wild laughter along with him, spread over that supple body and round melon-ass, cock shoved to the balls in a tightly twitching hole. He twisted the handle under his glove and a violent increase in speed had the front wheel leaping off the pavement briefly before slamming down and squealing forward.

They flew over the deserted highway, sun overhead beating down on them, one atop the other, cock splitting hole, legs apart, wind whistling over their naked bodies in a dancing stroke of a thousand tantalizing fingers.

The Road Rider fucked his bitch. Legs on either side of the sleek bike he loved, he pounded that lush ass for all he was worth. He was getting paid for the service, one more of the exciting jobs he was lucky enough to have, and he wasn't about to provide less than the ultimate in satisfaction.

Billy Macleod, tycoon of the largest company in the world, got fucked. The machine between his legs hummed and vibrated in a savage rhythm. The Road Rider who mounted him twisted and rolled the bike in a swaying and dizzying dance over the abandoned highway, both frightening and electrifying him.

Huge cock plunged in and out of his straining asshole. Tight as it was, he loved the feel of big cock stretching the muscle and banging inside against his sensitive prostate. The burrowing crown battered deep inside his guts. His own cock rubbed and slid over the smooth leather seat beneath him in a constant tease.

His plump ass gaped wide in that position, on his face, legs over the body of the bike, thus rendering him helpless to close them. He had to take that cock, whether he wanted to or not. He'd never been fucked like this.

Dason slam-drilled the increasingly pliant fuckhole between those sweet melon-cheeks. He reveled in the gradual surrender of that snug sphincter, twisting his hips as he swayed the bike over on its side to thrill them both, slamming deep as he revved up the speed and pulled back to lift the front wheel, thrusting deeper as the bike slammed back down onto the pavement.

The blond's supple arms stretched down alongside Dason's, his smaller hands gripping the Road Rider's large wrists. They were totally entwined, draped over the speeding bike, men and machine one.

With all that cock pummeling his prostate, and his own cock sliding back and forth over the smooth leather under him, it was no wonder Macleod came first. Drool flew off his plump lips as he shrieked against the roar of the wind and humped the seat under him. As cock plowed his ripe butthole from above, he thrust into the vibrating bike under him. He fucked it as he got fucked.

"I'm shooting! Your biker bitch is blowing a load, mate!"

Nut cream erupted all over the seat under them. Dason let out a whoop of triumph and increased their speed to a dizzying tempo. The hole surrounding his drilling cock clamped and convulsed in a wild dance as his blond client unloaded.

The realization that his bike was getting creamed only galvanized him to fuck more savagely. He rammed in and out, rolling the bike over from side to side expertly, dancing from one side of the road to the other, thrusting into the warm ass under him relentlessly.

"I'm creaming you, bitch!"

Orgasm was ripped out of him. Heart racing and lungs heaving, he gasped for breath as the Egyptian landscape flew past them in a blur. Cum spurted deep in his client's warm gut. He rode it out, slowly decreasing their frantic pace until they were once more throttling along sedately.

He engaged the motionaries and they rose up and back. Supine again, Macleod rested his helmeted head against Dason's broad chest. His cock dripped cum, but amazingly, was still rock hard up against his pale, freckled belly.

"You'll get your chance to make me the bitch, don't worry. You're paying enough for the privilege," Dason shouted in his ear, ticking the lobe with a big lick.

That evening he kept his promise. After a pit stop and lazy afternoon siesta beside a languid pool and swaying palms, they mounted again. This time Macleod threw his legs over behind Dason rather than in front.

It was the smirking Road Writer's turn to feel stiff cock tease his parted asscrack for a few languid hours. He leaned back against the supple warmth of his client's chest, thighs straddling his beloved bike, asscrack sliding over the stiff length of pink poker behind him. His own cock reared up fat and ready at his crotch, a fact Macleod took advantage of, with both arms around him and stroking in a lazy tease.

The red sunset waned and stars came out. The air cooled and blew briskly across them. It was Dason's turn to rise in his seat and settle back down over the rearing boner behind him. With a shout in the darkness, he gutted himself with the longest cock he'd ever taken.

He stood in the footpads and throttled up the bike, headlight illuminating empty highway ahead, the glowing eyes of wildlife scattering, and the dark waters of the Nile beside and below. He rode that cock behind him, slowly rising and falling over it to take more and more and more. It seemed like he'd never get to the root!

But he did. When he finally felt that impossibly long poker banging up against his lungs, he engaged the motionaries and once more they were thrown forward. With a leaping squeal, they lunged ahead, facedown, one atop the other, both clamping their thighs around their machine as men rode bike and cock rode ass.

Macleod gave as good as he got. He fucked Dason's hungry asshole with pounding glee. Dason moaned nonstop as he embraced his beloved bike and fucked it, his cock slippery under him as it slammed against the smooth leather seat. He arched his back and raised his muscular butt to take all the cock it was offered, crack wide open and clinging asslips throbbing.

The stars wheeled above as time passed. The fuck lasted and lasted. Dason was in heaven, naked body draped over his humming machine, warm flesh blanketing him and stiff, lengthy cock drilling his tender asshole and prostate. He slowed them down to a glide, the wind a soft caress rather than a howling blast. Macleod fucked with a slower, almost gentle pump. The sensation of flying through the night, through the stars, encased them in an eerie reality. His asshole succumbed to the hour-long battle to become a squishy sump for Macleod's pleasure. His own cock grew slick with lather beneath him.

When orgasm hit, it was shared in a simultaneous release. Dason felt his own goo spew in a slow pump of ecstasy, while his squishy asshole accepted the same. Macleod's tongue bathed his neck in wet swipes as they moaned around their orgasms.

They rode on through the night, one atop the other, bike between their thighs, cum and sweat shared.

"Don't stop till the sun comes up, mate. This is paradise."

Dason agreed.

They rode on.

# BLACK AND BLUE

## Rob Rosen

It was lunchtime. Naturally, he caught my eye. I mean, come on, the guy was hard to miss. Downtown, everyone was on his break; I was surrounded by businessmen in suits, jackets, ties, me included. And then there was him, in denim, friggin' snug too; heavy boots, scuffed; well-worn T-shirt, equally snug; black leather jacket. He was a big dude, thick in all the right places. Still, it was those eyes of his that pulled you in and wouldn't let go. They were startlingly blue, bright beneath the restaurant lighting, sparkling, standing out against all that slicked-back, jet black hair, and the sideburns running down his chiseled, scruffy cheeks.

Fuckin'-A, the guy was testosterone incarnate.

He sat alone, off to a corner, a square peg in a round hole. Speaking of which, mine was twitching just looking at him. Along with instant lumpage in my Armani slacks. *Boing.* So, yeah, when he got up to use the restroom, I followed, drawn like a moth to a blazing flame.

It was a small john, with two urinals and a crapper. He stood to the right, taller than me by a couple of inches, wider by a good twenty solid pounds, legs spread apart, the stream quickly flowing. I moved in next to him, separated by a foot of space, all air, no dividers. Thank you, absentminded architect.

I whipped my prick out and let 'er rip, glancing down out of the corner of my eye for a look-see. And, man oh man, even soft, it was long and thick, dangling down from within his mitt of a grip.

"Impressive, ain't it," he half whispered, half growled.

My heart beat out a samba in my chest. I guess my glance had turned into a stare.

"Oh," I coughed, that wandering eye of mine again staring straight ahead at the wall tile. "No. I, mean, yes. I mean, um, sorry."

He chuckled, his piss now over and done with, cock still in hand.

"What are you sorry about? You should see it at full mast." The last two words had an edge to them, something other than friendly bathroom banter.

I turned to look at him, his eyes suddenly on mine, like two lasers boring on through.

"Here? Now?" I gulped, eager if not utterly terrified.

He pointed to the enclosed can to our left.

"There. Now."

I quickly finished the task at hand and followed him over, both cocks still dangling, mine with a noticeable lift. He shut the door behind us, the sound echoing in the small enclosure. He shoved me up against the cold metal, the force making me jump, then wince, his body suddenly flush with mine, his hand grabbing my jaw, our eyes now an inch apart.

Somebody else entered the bathroom. My newfound buddy

held a vertical finger to his lips, a smile stretching wide across his face, his mouth suddenly on mine, rough, insistent, as we heard the other dude start to piss. His tongue darted out, snaking around mine, our pricks rising, pressed together, warm pulsing flesh on warm pulsing flesh. Our eyes stayed open, locked, watching, waiting.

Our unseen neighbor left us alone again and the guy's face suddenly yanked away, leaving my mouth throbbing from our brief contact. I looked down to see his cock now jutting out like a limb, eight steely inches of thick meat, veined along the shaft, the wide helmeted head dripping, glistening beneath the fluorescent lights.

"Man," I groaned.

Again that chuckle of his, gravelly, like pebbles tossed at the shoreline.

"Careful, it senses fear."

I sunk to my knees, fear not even near the top of the list of the things I was feeling, falling far behind lust and craving—a heady mixture, to be sure. He grabbed the beast and sent it swinging, slapping it up against my face in a dull *thud* before coaxing it inside my mouth, sending a happy gagging tear cascading down my cheek. He groaned as he pumped away, staring down at me, each inch disappearing, then reached for the back of my head, shoving my mouth down and around, his dick in and out.

"Fuck, yeah," he growled. "You're good at that."

Truth be told, I could suck like a Hoover. I winked up at him, popping his prick out for the briefest of seconds.

"Years of practice." Then I went back to work, slicking up his rod with copious amounts of spit as he once again rammed it inside my waiting mouth.

"Practice makes perfect," he added, suddenly pulling out, echoing my wink with one of his own, a smirk thrown in for good measure. "What else are you good at, I wonder?"

"Try me," I readily replied, saliva dripping down my chin.

He paused, then nodded suddenly, sadly cramming his prick back inside his jeans.

"Meet me on the corner at six." He bent down, the kiss this go-round gentler, his hand on my cheek for a caress and then a light slap. "Don't be late."

He unlocked the door and left, me still on my knees, still working my cock. I stopped pumping, figuring my jizz would find a better destiny soon enough.

"I won't be," I whispered, though he was already gone.

I waited a second, catching my breath, regaining my senses, then followed in his wake. I sat down at my table as he paid his tab and left, not even a smile or a wave good-bye. A minute later, I heard the roar of a motorcycle. I turned my head toward the sound as he flew by, black shades and matching helmet now added to his ensemble.

Six o'clock couldn't come soon enough. Then again, it didn't have much choice. Neither did I. In other words, he found me on the corner right on time, handing me a helmet and motioning for me to hop on the back of his Harley.

I hesitated but only for a moment. He dropped his shades, those eyes of his drawing me in like the ocean on a hot summer's day. I put the proffered helmet on and climbed in behind him, my hands instinctively around his waist, my front pressed up tight to his back as we zoomed away to points unknown.

The bike sent a vibration up my thighs and zigzagging across the rest of my body, the snarl of the engine the only sound I could hear, however muffled it was by the helmet. My hands moved in, from waist to belly, stroking his abs through the cotton of his shirt, moving up to tweak one nipple, then the other, both with noticeable bars through them. When we hit the first light, he pulled the shirt up and shoved my hand in.

"Your ass is mine," he hollered over his shoulder.

*Like duh*, I said to myself, my fingers exploring his torso, hard muscle, soft skin, all covered in a fuzzy down. I placed my chin on his back, hands roaming up and down, his thick nipples soon caught between my thumbs and index fingers, which pulled and kneaded, his own body now trembling even more than the Harley.

City gave way to town, town to country, the miles whizzing by with the breeze, the buzzing and humming of the machine below us lulling me into a glorious stupor, the aroma of gas and grass, of cow manure and flowering trees wafting languidly up my nostrils. He pulled off on a side road, out in the middle of nowhere, the motorcycle coming to a sudden halt behind a long-unused shed, nothing but untended fields in the distance. It was just him and me, alone.

"Off," he said, our helmets already removed as I hopped down first, him a second later, both of us standing face-to-face. "I meant your clothes."

A flush of crimson spread from cheek to cheek.

"Here?" I faltered, melting before his unflinching gaze. "You're, um, not going to fuck me and then kill me, are you?" I asked, only half joking. Maybe a quarter.

He laughed, a lurid twinkle to his eyes.

"Fuck, yeah; kill, no. Now off."

I did as he said, shucking off my Pradas, unrolling my dress socks, and setting them both on the grass. He stared down at me, arms akimbo, legs apart. I grinned nervously and unbuttoned my shirt, top to bottom, pulling the material out of my pants before adding it to my socks and shoes. Then came my undershirt, a warm breeze flowing over my exposed chest, my nipples suddenly eraser-tipped, rigid. His smile mirrored my own, his hand reaching out to explore my peaks and valleys; then he gave a slap across my chest, two down my belly. I winced and groaned, simultaneously.

"Pants. Hurry," he rasped.

So hurry I did, yanking off my belt, unbuttoning the top button, sliding down the zipper, and then shimmying out of my slacks, standing there in my tenting boxers, my cock straining at the silk. I looked up at him: he had a hungry look plastered across his rugged face, like he was a wolf who hadn't eaten in days, weeks.

"Hurry," he repeated, the word coming out in a low, deep exhale.

The boxers were slid down and off, leaving me naked, hard, my cock sticking out like a divining rod, the tip shiny with precum. He crouched down, pushing my legs apart, his hand reaching up and between, his fingers seeking and quickly finding my hole as his face leaned in for a sniff of my balls, his mouth engulfing my prick whole down to the hilt in one easy glide.

"Better," he sighed, in between hungry sucks and slurps and gulps, his digits pushing and prodding at my chute.

"Almost," I moaned. "Better would be if you were naked, too. Actually, *best* would be if you were naked, too."

He popped my prick out of his mouth.

"Certainly easier to fuck you that way."

I grinned, my hand stroking his mop of hair.

"I'd imagine so."

He stood back up, moving a foot away, his jacket, boots and thick socks all finding their way next to mine, then his T-shirt, revealing what I'd already felt, a densely muscled body, a black matting of fur, a six-pack with a seemingly extra set of cans. I stroked my cock as I watched his progress, his jeans quickly off exposing thick tree-trunk legs, hairy, well-worked calves. Then the briefs were slid down and off, leaving us both naked, rock hard, dripping.

He moved in, slapping my prick and sending it springing to and fro, then giving me a quick kiss, deep, perfect, before he veered right, his elbows on top of the bike's seat, his meaty, hairy ass jutting out, legs apart, lemon-sized balls dangling down.

"Eat it," he commanded.

Naturally I obeyed, crouching down, face to ass-level, spreading his cheeks apart, revealing a pink, crinkled, hair-rimmed hole winking out at me, beckoning me in. I leaned forward for a cursory lick, then a suck, my tongue making loops around the ring, the smell of musk and sweat filling my nose as I dove in, reaming him out as I yanked on his heavy nuts.

He moaned louder, stroking his cock as he shoved his ass into my face.

"Fuck, yeah," he spat, loudly, the sound of his voice streaming out in all directions.

"Speaking of fucking," I mumbled, my face still buried up his crack.

Again he chuckled, the rumble rolling down his body and out through mine. "Good idea."

I stood up, moving a few inches back.

"Great, in fact."

We switched places, my body hanging over his bike, elbows and stomach pressed down on hot leather, head turned to the side, my reflection in the chrome like a fun-house mirror's. I listened as he ripped open a rubber packet and then felt his hands on my legs, spreading them wide, my hole exposed, soon wet with slick spit, his mouth licking and sucking at it, biting on the tender skin while he spanked my cheeks, eliciting a grunt with each heavy-handed swat.

"Fucking sweet ass," he told me, his free hand pulling down

on my nut sac, causing me to crouch even lower. "Time to impale it."

That was music to my ears. I pushed my ass out and waited for the onslaught, one hand reaching down to stroke my cock, the other to balance myself on his bike. He slapped his prick across my butt, gliding the head down my crack, butting it up against my portal.

"Knock, knock," he snarled.

"Come on in," I replied.

The laugh was followed by a slight push, a slap across a cheek, a million volts of electricity coursing up my spine, then a sharp inhale as he entered me, tearing me open with his billy club of a dick that worked its way inside, inch by thick inch. He paused, allowing me to grow accustomed to the intrusion, a slap here, a smack there, playing my body like a base drum.

I released my clench, and his cock immediately plodded forward, slowly, surely, evenly, perfectly, sweat suddenly dripping from my brow, cascading down my back as he filled my ass with all that glorious manmeat, the bike rocking with each thrust.

"Sweet *and* tight," he commented, almost there, almost.

"A real résumé booster," I quipped, rocking my ass, willing him the rest of the way inside of me, my cock throbbing in my grip as every nerve ending in my body went off like the Fourth of July.

One more spank, one more thrust, and he was in like Flynn, the breadth and width of him battering up against my farthest reaches, our moans and groans carried away on the breeze that flowed over us, two men, one machine, all united together, literally and physically—metal and chrome and leather and flesh.

He retracted his cock with an audible *pop*, then rammed it back home again. I groaned in a mix of both pleasure and pain, the former soon overcoming the latter each time he slipped it out and shoved it back in, always adding a slap across my ass, along with a "Fuck, yeah."

He quickened his pace, pump, pump, pumping, *wham*, steady as she goes, his massive cock pummeling away as he gripped my waist, and I, in turn, gripped my prick, matching his rhythm, coaxing the sap up from my swaying balls.

"Make me come," I managed, in between shallow breaths.

He chuckled.

"No prob." And then he let me have it, rocketing his steely dick inside, lightning-fast, piston-fucking me, until you couldn't tell where I ended and he began. I jacked my cock faster now, my head tilted back, eyelids fluttering, sweat cascading down my back and off my face, the leather seat now drenched as the sun made its dip on the horizon.

"Close," I panted.

"Amen," he added with a final shove, ramming against my granite-hard prostate.

And then we were there.

My body shuddered and quaked, the bike holding me up now more so than my trembling legs, and with one long, low, deep moan, I shot and shot and shot, my heavy load spewing out and down, pooling on the ground in a puddle of hot, molten cum, his cock still buried up my ass, filling me with his jizz, his groans like a bear's growl flowing all around me in an aural embrace.

We stood there like that, catching our breaths, until he pulled his prick out and turned me around, grabbing me up in his big arms, our sweat-soaked bodies held tightly, his lips on mine again, soft as a pillow, eyes still open, big and bright and insanely blue.

"Fucking hot," he eventually whispered into my mouth.

"Understatement," I replied, still holding on, my hands

roaming his muscle-dense back, playing with the tuft of hair above his ass.

"Gotta go, though," he added, with a heavy sigh, a final peck and a wink.

I nodded, both of us wiping off with his T-shirt, then getting dressed again, then back on the bike, the sweet smell of our success lingering, pungent. The machine roared to life, kicking up a cloud of dust as it sped off, past the fields, cows, farms and small towns, coming once more to a stop where our little adventure had begun, downtown now deserted, evening in full force.

I hopped off and handed him back his helmet. He turned and smiled, his hand on my cheek, a light pat against my face, the engine revving its final good-bye, and then he was gone, disappearing around a corner.

Out of sight, but far from out of mind.

After that, he haunted me, images of his brawny chest, fat cock, eyes like sapphires, all running through my mind in slow motion, day and night. But he was only a dream, no longer a reality. I walked by the restaurant each afternoon. Nothing. Every passing motorcycle made my head turn, then spin. Still nothing.

There was only one option left; I had to make my own reality. That's what drew me to the bank that day. I walked in, heart pounding, eagerness mixed with a fear of what I was getting myself into. I found the loan officer's desk and sat down. I read the nameplate, SAMUEL LIPSON. I was told he'd be there to meet with me in five minutes. I pictured a short guy in glasses, with a bow tie, reedy voice, thin lips.

What I got was none of the above, not fucking close.

He sat down and looked up, locking eyes with me. In a three-piece suit, with slicked-back jet black hair, clean shaven but for long sideburns, blue orbs the color of the late afternoon sky.

Him.

He smiled.

"Good morning, Mr. Jones," he said. "You're interested in a loan today?"

I coughed, my voice suddenly caught in my throat.

"Um, yes. For a, um, motorcycle. A Harley."

His smile went north.

"Good choice. You ride?"

My smile mirrored his, my pants suddenly tenting.

"Plan to. Do you?"

He leaned in, arms crossed atop his desk.

"Oh, yeah. I ride, all right, Mr. Jones."

"Really, Mr. Lipson? Maybe you can teach me, then. How to ride, I mean."

He nodded his head, a black lock of hair falling out of place, that chuckle of his sending an eddy of adrenalin through my belly and up my spine, bursting in my head. He grabbed the papers I'd already filled out and signed them without even looking.

"You've got your loan, Mr. Jones. As for the teaching thing, meet me on the corner at six." He reached out to shake my hand, lingering, his grip like a vise. "And don't be late."

I laughed, sliding my palm across his.

"I never am, Mr. Lipson." I stood up to leave. "I never am."

# STURGIS BANG

## Logan Zachary

Tight jeans hugged his body and displayed his assets in their best light. The middle seam rode his crack, and a stress hole at his wallet pocket revealed that he wore no underwear. A hairy asscheek peeked out.

I hurried my pace to see if I could check out his basket.

He stopped and turned. His button fly strained as the outline of his cock stood proudly out in front. His leather vest exposed a hairy chest. His treasure trail was wide and funneled into his Wranglers.

My mouth opened as my tongue licked my dry lips. My eyes bore into his.

It was the first week in August, and the Sturgis Bike Rally was underway.

"Ex-excuse me, but do you know where the Buffalo Chip Campground is?"

Black sunglasses covered his eyes. A thick mustache covered his upper lip while a heavy five o'clock shadow added texture to his face.

"Follow the signs," his whiskey-soaked voice said, and he turned and walked away. I savored each swagger of his hips. What a way to start South Dakota's greatest tradition. A cold beer would be perfect right now. The low rumble of a pack of motorcycles hurried me to the side of the road. Dust and exhaust swirled in the air, pushing my body to find that cold brew.

"Dylan, are you ready to check into the campground?" Alex asked. "And then we can hit the beer tent."

Forcing my gaze to release the departing Wranglers, I turned to Alex and motioned. "The Buffalo Chip..."

"I know the way, Nurse Dylan, and the guy you tried to pick up will probably be staying there too, needing his pulse taken or something."

Alex's air-conditioned Jetta was a far cry from a hog, but it carried us to the Buffalo Chip in comfort. As we rode through the campground looking for our site, women in Daisy Duke shorts and bikini tops milled around. A few were topless and men stared openly at the views. Shirtless guys held beer cans and bottles as they leered at all the eye candy, unaware that they were eye candy for others.

"Anything goes here," Alex said, as he pointed at an elderly woman, who walked by with a dog's face painted on her belly and her flat flopping breasts painted as its ears.

"You go, Grandma," Alex said.

The woman smiled a toothless grin and waved, making the puppy's ears waggle.

"I've seen it all now."

"You haven't seen anything yet. This is the daytime. Wait until the sun goes down, then you'll see some crazy shit."

Our tent was set up, and we headed off in search of beer. The sun beat down as the heat hit triple digits. Luckily, a Dakota wind blew, taking the edge off the temperature. The lack of rain made the grass brown and dry. Dust rose up with each step we took. It was easy to see why no open fires were allowed.

Black T-shirts with the sleeves cut off and jeans of all styles and brands covered most, while others' bare skin tanned in the blazing sun. Hard rock music blared from all directions, radios, boom boxes, and a stage somewhere in the campground. Sheryl Crow was back this year, along with Godsmack and Nickelback—a different headliner each night.

The Wrangler man appeared from the crowd and walked toward us. His black sunglasses obscured his eyes, so I wasn't sure if he was looking at me or someone else. I smiled as he neared.

"Found it," I said, more to myself than to him.

He bumped into me as he passed, not even acknowledging my presence.

Alex grabbed my arm.

"He wants you. I can tell. It's the social worker in me, I'm helping you be social."

"He didn't even see me."

"He saw you. Why else would he brush up against you? He wanted to feel your body, make contact."

As he passed, it did feel like his hand traced along my thigh, caressing my leg, reaching for my...

"Dylan's in love, Dylan's in love."

"Lust, maybe, but not love. Not yet."

Barbecued ribs and chicken, corn on the cob, corn dogs, beer, nachos, everything was available. My ears rang from the loud music, my stomach was stuffed with food, and my bladder was bursting.

"I'm heading to the john and then I'm going back to the tent. I just need a little down time."

"Calling it a night already? It's not even eleven."

"No."

"Meeting Mr. Wrangler?"

"I wish. I'll be back. I'll text you when I'm heading back."

"You want me to go with you?"

"I'll be fine," I said, and took off before Alex decided to leave early also.

The low rumble of motorcycles echoed through the campground even this late at night. The smell of exhaust hung in the South Dakota breeze, but since sunset, the evening had cooled off.

I stumbled into my campsite and rifled through my tent, looking for my toothbrush. I walked to the bathroom and entered the concrete building. Quickly I relieved myself and washed up. Stepping back out into the night air, a low bass beat echoed from everywhere. There would be little sleep tonight.

Instead of heading back to the concert or the tent, I decided to enjoy the night air. A row of trees and shrubs blocked the view of the back area of the campground. The path led me farther into an isolated grove, cut off from the rest of the Buffalo Chip. The area appeared empty until a match flared to life, and a man's face was illuminated for a second as he lit his cigarette. Movement danced in the shadows of the trees.

"Hello? Is someone there?" I asked.

Several men stepped forward and approached me.

The man with the cigarette took a long drag on it, as the end burned a bright red. As he exhaled, the smoke circled his head.

"He looks like a Sturgis virgin to me."

Two men moved closer to me and grabbed my arms.

"Maybe he wants to learn the ropes of the biker rally."

Another man stepped forward with rope. I pulled away, but the men held me fast. The smoking man finished his cigarette and squished it out under his foot.

"Guys, that's not the way to entertain a guest. Offer him a beer."

A shirtless man with a red do-rag on his head opened a cooler and retrieved a Bud. He step in front of me and shook the can. He popped the top and a cold spray showered my face and shirt.

"Sorry, Sonny," the man said. He held the can to my mouth and poured the rest of its contents down my throat. What I couldn't swallow ran down my chin and soaked the rest of my shirt.

"Peter, how clumsy can you be?" Sonny said.

"Sorry," he said to Sonny.

"He's the wet one, not me. Apologize to him."

My whole body pulled back as he turned to me.

He reached into his pocket and pulled out a knife.

"Here, let me get that wet shirt off you." He grabbed the front of my black T-shirt and slid the knife up. Material ripped as the cool night breeze blew over my damp chest. He cut the sleeves and pulled the rag off my body.

Now, I wasn't embarrassed to take my shirt off at the pool, but when there were five men staring at me and one with a knife, I wanted to cross my arms over my chest and cover myself. A diamond of brown hair rested between my nipples. The hair started again as a triangle thickened across my abs and disappeared into my jeans.

"He has some hair, so he's not a little boy."

Peter's hand ran down my pecs to my belly button. Despite the fear I felt, my cock started to harden. I could feel the blood rush to engorge it. Sonny smiled a crooked grin. "He's not a little boy at all." He pointed to my growing arousal, and the other men laughed.

"The more to play with," Peter said. He ran the flat side of his knife along my shaft, which seemed to grow at the touch. He and Sonny noticed my body's reaction. The man with the rope wound an end around one of my wrists. The other two men pulled me over to the trees and tied it to a trunk.

I kicked and twisted, trying to break free, but the rope was secure. The man moved to my other wrist. As I opened my mouth to yell, Peter stuffed a piece of my beer-soaked T-shirt inside. He pulled at the material and tore off a long strip to wrap around my head. With ten hands pulling and tying, my legs were bound to the trees in seconds.

I stood spread-eagled between two trees as the men backed away to regroup. Swallowing hard, I wondered if Alex would come looking for me and would he find me. Sonny and Peter looked at each other and smiled. Sonny nodded and Peter readied his knife and drew near. My heart pounded in my chest as I started saying my prayers. Peter knelt at my foot and slipped the blade under my cuff. He took a few slices and the material split. My white sock came into view as he continued up my leg. My knee peeked out of the cut as Sonny stepped forward. Peter moved to my other leg as Sonny grabbed the two ends of the cut denim and pulled.

*RIP!* sounded up my left leg, and the night air raced up and swirled around my balls. I could feel them retract up against my torso, as my erection throbbed with each beat of my heart. My Calvins stretched against my arousal.

Peter cut up to my right knee, and Sonny stepped in front of me and looked into my frightened eyes. His hands slipped down the other side of my body as he held my gaze. His fingers played along my waistband, slid down over my erection, and found the ends of my pant leg and ripped it up to my waist. More night air rushed up.

I shook my head and screamed into my gag. My eyes pleaded,

but there wasn't anything more I could do.

"Ready for a night of fun?" Sonny asked. "We are."

His hands released the denim and let the long flaps dangle, then combed through the hair on my chest and his fingers circled my nipples. Each responded into tight sharp points.

"I see you are happy." Sonny pinched them.

Pleasure and pain burned through them. Sonny saw my response and pinched harder. He twisted my nipples, and my legs threatened to buckle.

Peter joined him. His knife's blade flashed as he neared. My skin prickled, afraid of being cut or worse. The sharp tip of the blade scratched down my abs. He pressed it there for a second and then lowered it under my waistband. With two quick cuts, he sliced through the waistband, and my jeans fell to the ground. The men behind me cheered. The Egyptian cotton was thinner than I wanted.

A hand caressed my ass, another touched my shoulder. Then I saw the look in Sonny and Peter's eyes—pure lust. Fingers pinched my bubble butt. One traced along my crease making the cotton stick to my sweaty skin. The back of my underwear was pushed up, giving me a wedgie as my ass was bared. A hand slapped my left cheek, and it stung.

"You'll all get your turn," Sonny said. "Just be patient."

Peter laughed. His hand ran down my stomach and explored my belly button. His index finger circled around and around, dropping in and out. It followed my treasure trail and stopped at the elastic waistband. His hand pinched the fat head of my cock and traced down the length of my shaft. He cupped my balls and squeezed.

Tears ran down my cheeks as I tried to kick and free myself. I screamed into my T-shirt, hoping it wouldn't slip down my throat and choke me.

*Alex, where are you?* my mind screamed as the others stepped closer.

Despite the fear, my body was excited—every nerve tingled and my arousal hurt as it strained against my briefs.

"Heads or tails?" Sonny asked Peter.

"I want both, but what would you like first?"

Sonny waved the other men away.

"Go and refill the coolers and get some ice. By the time you get back, we'll be done with him, and it'll be your turn."

The three reluctantly turned and headed to the pickup. The engine revved to life and the reverse lights came on. AC/DC blasted out of the windows as they drove away.

Sonny stepped behind me, as Peter moved in front. Sonny's hand patted my ass. His fingers dug through the underwear's leg holes and kneaded my ass, working their way to my crack. His thick fingers dug deeper and deeper.

Peter traced the elastic on my Calvins and combed down my treasure trail. With each of my breaths, he was able to get another fingertip under the strap. One finger found my mushroom head, precum pooled at the tip, and Peter's finger spread it.

"Give me the knife," Sonny demanded. He reached over my shoulder.

Peter pulled out of my underwear and handed him the blade. My buttcheeks pinched together as Sonny pulled on the fabric and cut. He pulled the cotton and ripped the ass out of my briefs. My exposed ass tensed in the night air.

Peter reached between my legs and pulled up on the front panel. My balls fell free from the pouch and dangled as my legs fought the ropes. His hands grabbed my testicles and milked them like he would a cow. He pulled and twisted hard, making me rise up onto my toes. Sonny threw my butt panel on the ground and spit onto his hand. He spread the saliva over his fingers and pressed them into my crease.

My body tensed and refused him entrance.

Peter's hand moved up from my balls and stroked my shaft. His fingers curled around me and squeezed. Precum oozed from my tip and flowed over his hand. Pleasure poured through me, and my legs relaxed.

Sonny, sensing the change, slipped his big finger between my cheeks and found my sensitive hole. His wet fingertip circled and probed, circled and probed as Peter's hand worked over my tender tip. My head fell back, and Sonny entered me with a strong stroke. His finger wiggled inside and the sensation made my body forget to struggle, and I just enjoyed the feeling.

Peter pulled the waistband up, and my dick sprang free.

Sonny pulled out of my ass and said, "I need more lube." He pulled my cheeks apart and leaned forward. He stuck his tongue out and entered me again. He spit out saliva with each penetration.

"How does he taste?" Peter asked.

He grasped my cock at the base and licked the tip. His tongue explored my slit and sucked the pearls of precum out. He opened wide as he took the head into his mouth. His tongue played along the underside of my cock as he swallowed it.

My furry balls bounced off his chin as he worked my eight inches.

I felt like a tennis ball volleying back and forth between Sonny and Peter. Their mouths and tongues worked over every inch of my moist sensitive flesh. And I fought with the same flesh, wanting to escape, but enjoying the ride.

Saliva ran down my ass and balls and continued along my legs. My testicles started to pull up alongside my shaft. A tingling pleasure started to rise and my hips started to seek out more. Peter's hand grasped me and pumped my dick as he worked me closer to a climax. He stood and unzipped his fly. His cock was hard, too. He had a thick black bush of hair above his seven-inch erection. He rubbed his dick against mine.

Sonny pulled his shirt off and worked his fly. He pulled out his cock and spat on it. He spread the spit down the length and moved closer. I could feel the big head slide along my ass. It plowed the row and explored, searching for the opening.

Peter's cock slid along mine and poked into my thick bush. A gooey wetness matted my hair together. Sonny's tip drilled into me and found my puckered hole. He pushed forward, hard, but couldn't enter. He backed up and tried again with more force. As Peter worked on my cock, I could feel my buttcheeks relaxing. Sonny's tip opened me wider, which encouraged his progress, and he surged forward, filling my sphincter.

Pain shot through me.

I could feel him slide farther in, as a shadow moved toward us. Peter turned and Sonny pulled out. I strained to see who was coming. The man approached, and Mr. Wrangler stepped into the light and everything stopped.

My abused body relaxed at the sight of him.

He walked over to me as Peter slipped behind me, covering his erection. Without a word, he reached up and took the gag from my mouth. I spit the wad of T-shirt out and swallowed hard. I licked my dry lips and smiled.

"Thanks," I croaked.

Wrangler reached up and ran his finger along the side of my face. He looked over my shoulder and said, "Why the hell did you start without me?"

My knees buckled. My rescuer was actually my abductor.

Wrangler reached down and grasped my semihard cock and stroked it. Despite the panic, my erection returned with a vengeance.

"Untie him and bring him back to the camper."

Sonny and Peter pulled up their pants and quickly untied me. Each took an arm and carried me to the camper. Wrangler opened the door and waited as the three of us entered. The back bedroom smelled like a locker room, hot humid air mixed with male sweat. The floor was littered with sleeping bags, pillows, blankets, condoms, and bottles of lube. Chains hung from the ceiling with a sling suspended from the ends.

Wrangler closed the door and followed. He grabbed the remains of my underwear and tossed them onto the floor. His hand caressed my butt and he motioned to the other guys. They spun me around and lifted me onto the sling. They secured my legs into the straps, spreading them wide open. My cock flipped up and flopped onto my belly. I could feel my balls slip down between my cheeks and rest on my tight hole. Wrangler stepped between my legs and grasped my cock.

"I'm glad you came looking for me. I've been looking for you."

I raised my head to watch him. His jeans were tighter than before, and something was definitely bigger. Sonny and Peter took off their pants and moved up to my head. Two erections stood straight out in front of them. I grabbed one in each hand and stroked in time with Wrangler.

"You got him ready for me," he said, unbuttoning his jeans. He wore no underwear, and his thick bush burst forth. His massive cock swelled once the pressure of his tight jeans was removed.

Sonny and Peter moved closer, pressing their cocks against my face. Sonny's uncut eight inches oozed a huge pearl of precum, which he spread over my cheek. I turned to face him, opening my mouth and sticking out my tongue.

Sonny took the welcome and placed his dick in my mouth.

My tongue curled and cupped his length. My hand grabbed his balls and squeezed. Another huge pearl of precum slipped out of his foreskin and spread down his shaft.

Peter's penis humped my hand.

Out of the corner of my eye, I watched Wrangler push down his jeans and his monster cock surged forward. His balls hung low and swung with his movement. He poured lube down his length and spread it over every inch.

He rubbed his length along mine, transferring the lube that dripped down both sides. He used his tip like a paintbrush, painting my balls and lubing my ass. He found my opening, circled the hole and explored it. He pressed in, testing the access.

My muscle relaxed, and I felt him start to enter me.

He ripped open a condom and slipped it on. Pouring lube over it, he stepped between my legs and positioned himself, ready for action. He smeared the overflow onto my cock.

Sonny pulled out of my mouth and Peter pressed forward. I turned to face him and his cock entered my mouth, but before I could swallow, his balls were bouncing off my chin. Sonny moved so my hand could keep up the rhythm.

Wrangler knelt down, working his hard cock along the way. His tongue trailed down my shaft. His lips puckered and kissed my dangling balls, which he sucked into his mouth and rolled one by one between his teeth. My testicles started to pull up against my torso. I could feel my buttcheeks spread wide and lubed, ready for Wrangler. He licked the puckered muscle and it pulsated under his tongue. He licked in circles and slipped to the opening, seeking entry. He pressed against the smooth muscle, slowly digging in deeper and deeper.

Peter's cock pounded my mouth as saliva dripped down my chin. He humped me faster and faster. His strokes went deeper and deeper, and then he pulled out. Sonny moved closer, straddling my arm.

Musky male sweat greeted my nostrils as I breathed in deeply, savoring the true masculine scent. My head was lined up, and Sonny slipped his dick in my mouth. Peter, seeing Sonny's position, copied it and had his cock alongside Sonny's. Each man took turns entering me. Their cocks slipped against each other as they leaned forward to kiss. Their tongues played back and forth.

Spit poured out of my butt as Wrangler inserted one finger. He wiggled it around and slowly pushed it in and out. I moaned with pleasure as both ends of my body were penetrated. My balls pulled up higher along my shaft. Wrangler jacked my cock with his fist, as his other hand tried to push two fingers inside me. His thick ten-inch cock bounced with his motions. He twisted and turned inside me, making me ready for his giant dick.

Sonny's and Peter's penises continued to rub against each other as they took turns entering my mouth.

Wrangler pulled his tongue out of me and grabbed his erection and aimed it into me again. His swollen head bull's-eyed my opening and drove itself in to the hilt. His furry balls bounced off my butt, as his hand stroked my hard-on and milked it. He pulled his shaft out and drove it back in. His rhythm pounded steady and even. My hands and mouth worked at the same pace. My balls tingled as desire rose deep inside me. Wrangler filled me with his girth, stretching and stimulating me as he drove in and out. His balls slammed against my butt, the tip pounded my prostate gland, starting spasms of joy flowing through my body.

His rate increased, and I squeezed harder on the cocks in my mouth. Wrangler's finger explored the opening on my cock. He spread the precum down my shaft and quickened his stroke. My body spasmed and exploded with pleasure. My ass clamped down on his dick as he thrust inside and I felt his body go rigid. He slammed against me and stayed rooted there, humping me with violent bursts as he came.

My hands grasped tight and soon my fingers and mouth filled with thick, salty cream. Wave after wave of cum flowed over me and into me, dripping between my fingers and down my chin. Wrangler continued to jack my penis and my whole body reacted. My ass tightened and pushed him out. He yelled in pleasured pain as his sensitive cock exited my tight hole. Sonny and Peter pulled away from my grasp, which wouldn't let go. Their bodies fell backward, and I released them before I ripped something off. They collapsed on the floor whimpering.

No one moved for several minutes as our heart rates and breathing returned to normal.

Wrangler helped me out of the sling and threw a hand towel to me. I wiped off as much as I could, but the towel wasn't absorbent enough to soak up all the cum.

"How am I going to get back to my tent?" I asked as I handed him the rag.

"You're close, I'm sure you can walk that far," Wrangler said with a grin.

"But all my clothes were..."

"No one will even notice you. You've seen some of the wild shit that goes on around here."

I shrugged my shoulders as I exited the camper. My bare feet slipped on the morning dew. The night was giving way to morning, as the sun tried to peek over the horizon. I snuck across two campsites and ran through a grove of trees and bushes. I passed a picnic table with a guy lying on his back buck naked as another guy was giving him a blow job. Neither one noticed a naked man running past.

I slipped into the tent and found my sleeping bag.

"Did you have a good night?" Alex asked.

Flopping down on my back, I exhaled loudly.

"Ahhhh, I had a blast."

"I'm glad you made some new friends."

I smiled to myself.

"I did, I made some great new friends, and they want to meet you, tonight."

# NUMBER 023 OF THE 200 MADE

### Derrick Della Giorgia

I t was that time of the year again.

Early May in Rome is something that hits you in the face, a change of seismic violence, a pharmaceutical mixture that seizes your senses for at least a couple of weeks before you get used to it. It is just as hard for me to explain as it is for you to understand, unless, of course, you've experienced it.

The air is sweet again, liquid on your skin—like the warm water you wash your face with during winter. The flowers are back in the streets and the green is on the trees, people walk on the sidewalks where the sun doesn't reach and wear less clothing. Miniskirts, flaccid square necks, bosoms and legs on high heels are again the main causes of car accidents, and invisible birds sing all day long.

This alone would be enough to shake a boring routine, but the detail that makes me lose grip of my dignity—literally—was another one. Early May in Rome brings out in the streets the species I like the most: young rich guys on their bikes. They aren't the ones who use their bikes to go to work or to move through the futuristic dirty traffic of the capital. They put on their Lacoste polo shirts, their Prada shorts, Gucci flip-flops and Hermes sunglasses and look for fun. I hate bikes, but their owners' soft skin in the sun makes me wish I was a mechanic!

It was that time of the year again in Rome, but this time it was different. I met Basilio in April, when I dropped the green olive of my dirty Martini on his Burberry jacket at Freni e Frizioni, a typical Roman *aperitivo rendez-vous*. My friends laughed, shamelessly; his friends worried for the jacket, seriously. I don't remember how we got past my excuses and his fake noncha-lance, but three drinks later we were still talking, our respective friends leaving one by one. His namedropping of iPhone and many more bourgeois marks didn't stop me, thanks to his light green eyes that matched the color of the muddy Tiber waters behind him. There was a wave of outdatedness and relaxation about him, with a kick of almost childish devilment that kept me riveted to his words until the streetlamps on the sides of the river went on and the sky turned black above us.

"How are you going to make me forgive you, philosopher?" Basilio asked. My reflections on life amused him and he had coined that nickname for me. He pushed his index finger into my chest and smiled, with his lips first, then with his whole face.

"Are you still trying to accuse that little olive of destroying your jacket?" I asked. The liquor stain wasn't visible anymore, and he couldn't even remember which side it had fallen on.

"All right. How about...I pick you up next Friday with my new Vespa and we take a ride on the Appian Way? I just got it delivered from the U.K. It's the limited edition Vespa Zafferano. Mine is number twenty-three of the two hundred made."

*Another gadget the baby needs to show off,* I thought.

"Sure, I'd love to try your new toy." I rolled my eyes and he didn't like it. He spent the last ten minutes of our conversation breathlessly trying to convince me that his bike was unique and deserved respect—that it meant a lot to him and that the only reason why he'd offered to let me try it was I was an interesting and intriguing person. Ten long minutes of nervous gesticulating and concentrated mechanical information.

"What time should I come?" he asked, then answered for me: "I'll pick you up at three. May is the best time to drive down the queen of the long roads!" Basilio left me with that Latin citation, raising my interest in what hid under his designer clothes and my tolerance for his expensive and limited-edition jewel.

We met at the Aurelian Walls, under Porta Appia, at 3:00 P.M. as he had insistently suggested. I arrived earlier and hid under the arch to save myself from the already aggressive Roman sun. The air was cool and thicker under the ancient tunnel, the silence anticipating the peaceful and timeless atmosphere on the road that ended in Brindisi, more than 500 kilometers south of Rome in Apulia.

When I saw him, my theory about May, Rome and rich guys on their bikes came to mind and I knew I had scored. Preceded by the roar of his Vespa Zafferano, he showed up from inside the walls that enclosed all the seven hills of Rome, and halted two feet away from my right knee, which I had teasingly bent while resting against the wall. He turned the bike off and pushed his sunglasses back into his hair, messed up by the wind during the ride. Of course the helmet wasn't fashionable enough for him and he had it hung from his elbow instead of on his head. His legs were elegant and his thighs well exercised. He looked enthusiastic.

"So, don't you love it?" he asked, his facial features relaxed, waiting for his desire to be quenched by my words.

"What?" I said, knowing perfectly well he meant the damn

bike, but couldn't he have said, *Hi, how are you* or *Nice to see you* first?

"My Vespa Zafferano! This is only the second time I've used it. Did I tell you there are only two hundred of these babies and mine is number twenty-three?"

"Cute," I said.

I couldn't believe I was jealous of a bike. The thing was a cheesy Halloween orange and—as he explained without being asked—came with two unique black stripes on the sides and a couple of other ultraspecial items I didn't have the attention span to listen to. After a cigarette and almost half a bottle of water, Basilio finally came closer and greeted me. The conversation became more appropriate, and he suggested I get on the bike behind him so we could start the journey. His gentle way of moving turned me on, and I decided to get over the initial nonsense.

"Wait a second!"

He blocked my waist when I was about to mount the metal pumpkin. I could tell there was something completely wrong.

"What?" I asked.

"Your flip-flops are leather..."

This time I didn't need any explanation. He was terrified I was going to scratch the varnish.

"I'll be careful. Don't worry."

I moved an inch and he trapped me in his arms, his head nested into my chest.

"No! Please! Please! Please! Take them off, I beg you..."

I complied. With my bottle of Ferrarelle in one hand and my hazardous leather flip-flops in the other, I hugged his tight waist and enjoyed the view. The sun reflecting off his white linen collar shirt blinded me, and the bumpy noisy ride dampened the rest of my senses. Nevertheless, it was amazing. The curious trees that jutted in the air above us set our path, and the perfume of plants and stones combined with the one descending on my face from his neck, making me wish we'd never stop. Five long and unforgettable miles went by.

"I want to take you to Villa dei Quintili..." he announced and quickly kissed my lips when I parted them to answer him. I had never gone that far down on the Appian Way, but it sounded like it wouldn't be his first time.

"Take me wherever you want," I whispered into his ear and tightened my embrace. By the time he decreased our speed, my hands were intertwined right above his cotton shorts. He carefully spotted the most beautiful view and slowly stopped.

"Why, why, why did you have to die on my Vespa?" Basilio said as soon as he got off the Vespa and inspected the front of the bike.

"What now?"

"This huge bee decided to die on my baby. Look! All the juice that came out of her..." He frantically changed position at least three times to get the best angle and then extracted his handkerchief and knelt on the ground to polish the tiny spot. Meanwhile, I put my flip-flops back on, fixed my hair in the mirror and looked around.

"What's that over there?" I asked. Nested between the green of the grass and the cerulean sky, what looked like an abandoned village waited for us on top of a minuscule hill.

"That is Villa dei Quintili. I can't believe you've never been here before," he said. Smiling, he stretched his arm toward me, requesting my hand. Then he pulled me into his arms and started teaching me all he knew about the villa. Absurdly enough, the ancient ruins in the sun had acquired the same color as his Vespa and we perfectly matched in the picture.

"Do you want to go in there?"

"Do you?" My heart was still inebriated, and all I wanted was to have him.

"I am the happiest man on earth where I am right now." This time I didn't wait for him to take the initiative and kissed his spoiled lips. He pulled me closer and explored my neck with his tongue, biting me now and then to keep me alert. "I want to tell you a secret..." he continued.

"Let me guess, you want to make love on your number twenty-three?" I said. I kissed him again and mounted the Vespa, simulating an orgasm on the overheated saddle.

"Stop that!"

He was almost ridiculous now. He put his hands between my ass and the leather to protect it. "Please, get off..." He surely knew how to destroy the heat of a moment. "I was thinking of something different..." He put his hand in my pants and kept talking. "I would love to have a threesome."

"Sounds good. But I'm dying right now," I said. His face revealed his thoughts before he could utter a word. He looked so enthralled I was almost uncomfortable, but at the same time, sort of curious.

"Would you mind if my baby joined us?" he asked. He bent on his knees by the front tire—the second time in less than an hour—and wet the hot metal with his open mouth.

"Whatever turns you on, sexy!"

The idea didn't bother me. His submissiveness to an inanimate object played its trick. He took off his clothes and lay down on the grass by the tire in his underwear, rolling around and getting black marks all over his white smooth chest.

"Come join us..."

I threw myself onto him and started manipulating the round bulge that had formed in his Dolce & Gabbana briefs. His thighs were of the white you see in churches and his knees round and

aristocratic. Basilio was in love with his bike, and I was in love
with him. He jumped to his feet and voraciously licked the silver
mirror, offering me his ass. I peeled his briefs off of him and
admired the contents: hot, round, sweet butt, up high in the air
for me.

"Give it to me."

I possessed his ass like the Vespa was possessing him. I bit
him and sucked the tender spot next to his ball sac. It was then
that I saw his dick for the first time, dripping sticky nectar of
excitement on the fresh grass.

"I want to be inside of you," I said.

"You have to share me with her!" he laughed, mounting the
saddle and spreading his legs. "You can be rough with me, but
be gentle with her..."

I stepped in the middle of them, resting my back on the
handlebar, and banged my marmoreal dick on the leather he
cared so much for—one, two, three times, watching his body
writhing in pleasure. Then I made my way into his flesh passage
and I started my ride. The sun was a little lower now and didn't
bother our skin but enhanced the colors around us and made
us feel surreal. I pinned his waist down with both my hands
and dove deeper into him, obtaining from his mouth the well-
known sighs.

"Start her! Now!"

I followed his orders and enjoyed the lullaby of the motor
under my balls. The bike sounded more aggressive now, as if
actively participating in our fuck. He anchored himself to the
saddle and welcomed my precisely calculated thrusts with the
elegance of a gymnast. My calves kept working mechanically,
and the heat that our bodies produced beat the combustion in
the motor. I felt connected to the Vespa for the first time; my
orange accomplice forced my rich brat into position and lifted

his hips toward me with its powerful vibrations. There was no distance between the three of us and we moved harmoniously together.

"I'm about to blow!" I warned him while licking his red, panting mouth.

"Come on her! Please. She deserves it..." he begged, then spit me out of his ass and massaged my dick against the black soft leather until a white spurt drew a thick creamy line across the saddle and descended on the orange varnish. At that, Basilio's pupils widened in ecstasy and his dirty knees hit the ground again in religious respect. Both hands crammed in his crotch, he followed the rivulet of cum with his tongue and swallowed it all down, polishing his number 023 of the 200 made as he flooded the grass around the back tire.

# CHROME-OBSESSED

## Pepper Espinoza

The only thing Teddy liked more than the smell of leather was smooth, cool chrome beneath his fingertips. He knew he shouldn't touch the big Harley. If Howard Bell didn't kill him for fucking around with the bike, then his father surely would. How many times had they told him to stay away from the bikes? How many times had he been told that you never, *ever* touch another man's bike, unless you want the other man to lay you out with a fist to the face? Too many to count. That had been the story of his life ever since he had been a little boy. In fact, one of his earliest memories was of reaching for the shining chrome with chubby fingers—and having the same fingers slapped away with a harsh word. But even the promise of certain punishment wasn't enough to restrain him.

He bent over and inhaled deeply, capturing the combined scents of leather, Howard's body, gasoline, oil and dust. Howard lived on his bike, traveling from one side of the country to the other, and the smell made Teddy think of the open road. There was a whole world out there that Teddy couldn't even imagine, one that had never been accessible to him. The closest he ever got was when he started working in his father's garage off the highway. He provided an eager ear to many of the men who stopped there for parts, and if they had to work on some guy's bike for more than a day, Teddy happily provided more than just an ear.

Except for Howard, his father's closest friend and the man who had played the most prominent role in Teddy's fantasies since he was fourteen. Six years hadn't dampened Teddy's desire. If anything, the passage of time heightened it. Because the older he got, the more his wishes became a possibility. Howard would probably never see him as anything except Robert Digger's son, but his chances sure as hell improved once he turned eighteen. At least, that's what he told himself. But on the night after his twentieth birthday, the situation seemed as hopeless as ever.

Teddy hadn't bothered to lock the garage door behind him, but only because he didn't think anybody would bother following him out of the house. Howard and Robert were busy drinking and talking about the good old days—the really great ones before Robert married and got saddled with a kid—and everybody else had gone home for the night. Teddy had the garage, and Howard's massive Harley-Davidson Fat Boy, to himself.

He circled it, boldly letting his fingers trail along the seat, the gas tank, the big handlebars. The keys had been sitting in the office, and Teddy clutched them now, though he didn't know if he had it in him to actually start the engine. They would undoubtedly hear it, but there were plenty of bikes that Teddy could be working on in the garage. Besides, both of them were so drunk, they probably wouldn't even notice. From a distance, and through the haze of alcohol, even Harold's Fat Boy would sound much like any other Harley-Davidson.

Satisfied that he would not get caught, he slid the key into the ignition and turned it into position. Taking a deep breath, he threw his leg over the seat, straddling the beast. Even without the engine rumbling, he felt its power. His cock pressed against his jeans, aching for freedom. His hand strayed to his zipper, but he stopped himself. Not yet. Not until the engine vibrated beneath him, and the low growl resonated from his eyes to his toes.

His fingers were shaking as he started the engine. It roared in the small space, bouncing off the walls and the floor and the ceiling. Teddy closed his eyes in bliss. He didn't want to wheel it out of the garage. He didn't want to ride it over the open road. He didn't want to pretend he was Howard. He just wanted to absorb each vibration, the texture of the chrome, the smell of the exhaust into his flesh. Unable to resist for another moment, he unzipped his shorts and pulled his thick erection free.

Teddy shuddered at the first stroke of his shaft, his fingers catching the precum already soaking the crown. He couldn't remember the first time a Harley gave him wood. Maybe around the same time he first fantasized about Howard. Or maybe it was earlier than that. Maybe it was when he was twelve, and he had pointedly ignored his father and crawled on the back of a midnight blue Electra Glide while nobody was looking. Regardless of when it began, it was a fact of his life. There were copies of *Easy Rider* and *V-Twin* magazines under his bed instead of *Playboy* and *Penthouse*. The first guy he fucked had been covered in oil, smelling of gasoline and ugly as sin.

And now, finally, he sat on the bike that had been paramount in his dreams. Teddy jerked his length again, automatically pushing his hips forward. As he did so, the crown scraped across the smooth metal of the tank. A bolt of electricity shot down his spine, and he did it again without thought. The second time did nothing to decrease the thrill. In fact, it only made him more aware of how delicious it felt. Especially when he held his cock against the metal and let the motorcycle's vibrations flow through him.

It briefly occurred to him that he would need to wash the bike when he was finished, because he was going to shoot his load all over the tank. He shuddered with hunger at the thought of watching his own spunk roll down the sides of the tank, covering the Harley-Davidson logo emblazoned there. The thought had occurred to him before, but he had never really expected to be in the perfect situation for it.

With his prick trapped between his palm and the vibrating tank, he pumped his hips in a slow, deliberate rhythm. A voice in the back of his mind reminded him he didn't have all night, but he tuned it out. He didn't care that he should finish up and get out of there before he really pushed his luck—he had been waiting for this opportunity, for this moment, for far too long.

For a moment, he considered stripping down to nothing, not even an insignificant scrap of cloth coming between the two of them. He would feel the bike's heat right against his skin, contrasting sharply with the cool chrome of the handlebars, and the soft, worn leather seat. But that was going a step too far, and even in the haze of his arousal, he didn't want to be stupid.

Teddy closed his eyes, and the vibration against his balls sent sparks flying through him, erupting in the darkness. The tank was warming beneath his shaft, but it was nothing compared to the heat of his palm. It was dry and smooth, while his palm was already damp across the top of his length. Howard's wouldn't feel anything like that. Howard's hand was much larger, for one thing. And it was rough, weathered by the sun and the wind and too many years of riding without gloves. The calluses would scrape across his tender skin, smearing the slick precum, and his other hand would be hard on Teddy's shoulder, holding him in place. He would have no hope or chance of moving. Even when Howard tightened his grip, squeezing until real pain blossomed through his abdomen, Teddy wouldn't be able to move.

Teddy jerked his hips faster, his head falling backward. He was going to lose it. The motorcycle would cover the sound of his scream, and he was grateful for that. Because when he finally did bust a nut, he wasn't going to be quiet about it. He might give himself over to the fantasy completely and shout Howard's name.

He caught his bottom lip with his teeth, and his breath came in faster and faster gasps. He kept his feet planted firmly on the ground, but he wished he could straddle the bike properly. Thrusting his hips harder and harder, he smeared more of the clear liquid across the gas tank. It even caught on the edge of the seat. It covered his hand. The fumes from the exhaust made him feel more than a little heady, and he knew he needed to turn the bike off. He needed to open the door. He needed a blast of fresh air to make everything make sense again. But that would have to wait. The heavy, oily smell settled against the back of his tongue, coating his sinuses. He would still be smelling it that night when he finally went back to his own bed, still vibrating, still hard. Still aching for a touch he couldn't have....

Teddy gripped his cock, desperate for just a little bit more pressure, a little bit more friction. His balls pulled tight, and the base of his spine tingled. It seemed to match the vibration of the bike, and a hard wave of pleasure swept through him, tightening every muscle, making every nerve-ending flare to life. With a shout, he watched the cum shoot from his body, landing across the black paint in long, white strings.

"I hope you plan to clean that up."

Teddy froze, his cock shrinking in his hand. He didn't look around to meet Howard's gaze. His face and neck felt impossibly hot, and the pleasure that had been so intense just moments ago completely drained away.

"I...yes, sir..."

"Good."

All the metal on his boots and coat jangled as the man crossed the room. Teddy didn't even know how—or why—he could hear it over the roar of the bike. But he could hear the heavy soles of Howard's boots against the concrete as he approached. Teddy still didn't move. Not even when Howard reached over and turned the ignition off. The sudden silence was more deafening than the bike had been, and Teddy's heart hammered so hard in his throat, he thought he might choke.

"Well? What are you waiting for?"

"I...I'll grab a rag..."

"No, not a rag. I want you to use your tongue."

Teddy stared at him.

"I..."

"Use your tongue. Or would you rather I let everybody know what you've been doing in here?"

By *everybody*, Teddy had no doubt that he meant Teddy's father. And since that was the last thing he wanted, he bent at the waist, stretching his tongue to catch the dripping liquid. Howard held the back of Teddy's head, his hand even larger than Teddy had imagined. It felt like the older man could crush his skull, if he wanted to. And would he want to? The sick feeling at the center of his gut told him that this night probably would not have a good ending for him.

The liquid tasted vaguely metallic, vaguely oily. The metal was warm against his tongue, and Howard pressed on his head until his teeth clicked against the tank. He tried to look from the corner of his eye to see Howard's face, but the best he could manage was an eyeful of Howard's crotch—and his undeniable erection. The sight of it, combined with the salty flavor of his own cum, made his cock twitch.

"Don't stop. I want every inch of this clean."

Teddy closed his eyes and dragged his tongue along the edge of the gas tank, following the line like it belonged to a lover. Once the thought occurred to him, Teddy knew it was the right one. Shedding his previous hesitation, he licked back up the bike—clean of everything except his spunk. He worshipped it with his mouth, using more than just his tongue to clean it. He worshipped it like he would have worshipped Howard's body if it was the man stretched out in front of him. He worshipped the bike like it deserved. As he did so, his hunger grew. He would have happily covered the entire bike with his mouth, would have happily followed every curve of it, dipped his tongue into every crevice.

"You like this, don't you?"

What would be the point of lying about it?

"Yes, sir."

"You like the way the bike tastes? The way it feels?"

"Yes, sir."

"You're a sick little puppy, do you know that? Keep going. I didn't say you could stop."

"Yes, sir."

"You do this sort of thing with all the bikes in your daddy's garage?"

"No, sir."

"Really?" He squeezed Teddy's skull for a moment. "How do I know you're not lying to me?"

"I'm not, sir."

"Oh, I think you're probably not. So, what is it? You saw my bike and you just lost all sense of control?"

The tank was entirely clean of cum at that point, but Howard didn't let him lift his head. The tongue bath continued, and the smell of gasoline filled his head. Would he always link gasoline to that moment? Would he be able to fill up his car without getting a hard-on? Teddy suspected the answer to that question was no, especially since he wanted to beg Howard to never let go of him.

"I couldn't...I couldn't help myself, sir."

"Is that a fact?"

"Yes, sir."

"Because it's my bike?"

"Yes, sir."

The words were barely out of his mouth before he cried out with shock and pain. Howard's fingers were closed around his balls like a vise, squeezing him through the denim of his shorts. He didn't try to twist away—but only because he didn't want to risk tipping the bike.

"You like this, too?"

"I..."

"Don't lie to me, boy."

"Yes, sir."

"Get down off that bike. It's not yours."

As soon as Howard released him, Teddy scrambled off the bike. A hard hand on his shoulder forced him to the dirty floor. It put him eye-level with Howard's cock, and his erection seemed even more massive from that vantage. Every muscle in his body strained forward, and he wanted to close his mouth over the hard line and bite him through the thick denim.

"Get down on your hands and knees. Like a dog."

Teddy dropped forward without protest. His cock hung between his legs, poking out through his open fly. He wished he could tuck himself back in his pants. Or take off his shorts completely.

"You like the taste of dirt and oil so much? Lick my boots."

"Sir?"

"Lick them."

Teddy looked up through his lashes, staring at Howard's face, looking for any sort of sign. The man's features were impassive, his eyes small and impossible to read. Teddy lowered his head slowly, giving Howard ample time to tell him to stop, that he was just kidding, that this was ridiculous. But Howard didn't speak. He didn't move—not even a twitch. And Teddy had no choice but to lick the tip, wincing at the strong taste of the road—asphalt, and exhaust, and oil, and leather, and heat.

"Again. Lick the other one."

Teddy had no choice but to alternate between the boots, dragging his tongue across the toe before shifting his attention to the other side. Howard grunted each time he moved, and Teddy thought they were sounds of approval. Or maybe they were tiny exclamations of surprise. Surprise that anybody would allow himself to be debased like that. Surprise that anybody would enjoy it as much as Teddy obviously did. Surprise that he could get away with making his best friend's son so hard he could burst.

"Do you want me to fuck you?" Howard demanded.

"Yes, sir."

"Don't stop licking."

"Yes, sir," Teddy said, the words muffled by the motion of his tongue.

"Do you want me to fuck you on the bike?"

Teddy literally shook from the force of his hunger.

"Yes...yes, sir."

"Do you want *me*, or do you just want somebody who'll throw you over the back of the bike and tear your ass apart?"

"You...you, sir."

"Tell me."

"I want you to fuck me, sir."

"No, use my name."

"I want you to fuck me, Mr. Bell."

"Call me Howard."

Teddy finally looked up, daring to pull his mouth from the boots.

"I want you to fuck me, Howard. Please."

Howard bent and grabbed Teddy by the arm, hauling him to his feet. Howard had a good six inches on Teddy and was several inches wider, though his body was well-muscled instead of fat. His strength could be a little scary—well, a lot scary. He could pick Teddy up over his head and snap him in two. Yet, despite that, when he touched the side of Teddy's face, it was with undeniable tenderness, like it would never occur to him to do anything to hurt the younger man.

"Get out of those clothes. All of them."

Teddy stripped quickly, happy to shed his clothing. His gaze kept slipping to the bike. Was Howard really going to fuck him on top of it? He didn't dare hope for it to really happen, but he couldn't deny the way Howard looked at him. Or Howard's obvious arousal. Especially when the older man unzipped his pants and allowed his cock to spring free.

"Straddle the bike like you were. Grip the handlebars, and stick your ass in the air."

Teddy could barely walk, he was shaking so hard, but he did as he was told. His clammy hands closed around the plastic grips, and his cock dragged across the seat—once again wet with precum. Like he hadn't just shot all over the bike. Like he hadn't been touched in weeks. A part of him wanted to ask if he could start the bike again, but he knew instinctively not to make any requests. He didn't want to appear greedy, like he was taking more than he had the right to. He was already getting so much more than he had ever expected.

"God, look at this little ass."

Howard slapped a rounded cheek hard enough to make Teddy moan. "I bet you're tight for me, aren't you?" He dragged a finger down Teddy's crack, then pushed the tip past his pucker. The initial intrusion didn't exactly hurt, but it did burn. Teddy's fingers tightened on the plastic grips until his knuckles turned white, and even that was not enough to ease the fire sweeping through him. And that was just one finger.

"You haven't been fucked in a while, have you, boy?"

"No...no, sir."

"I can tell."

He pumped his wrist, sliding his finger in and out of Teddy's tight passage. Everything inside of Teddy twisted and turned, burning and melting together. If he shouted, would anybody hear him? If he called out Howard's name, would his father notice? Because the sound was building at the base of his throat, and he would do anything, anything at all, to relieve the pressure in his chest. He stared down at the bike and saw his own reflection in the chrome gas cap. His face was contorted with pleasure, and his blond hair flopped over his brow, partially obscuring his eyes. Even in the distorted mirror, he could see how red his cheeks were, how his eyes shined.

"You ready for more?" Howard asked gruffly.

"Oh, yes, sir. Please."

Teddy looked over his shoulder, watching as Howard fished his wallet out of his back pocket. It only took seconds for him to rip the foil open and slide the rubber down his length. He spit in his palm and stroked himself, spreading it and the condom's lubricant over his shaft.

"Hold on tight."

Teddy didn't need to be told to hold on. He did it automatically, his chest hitching with each breath, his palms slick with sweat. The head of Howard's cock was fat, and he worked it into Teddy's body with an amazing patience. Slowly, slowly, allowing Teddy ample time to adjust to the intrusion. He had no way to gauge just how much of Howard's cock was already inside of him—it felt like he was completely sheathed, and yet, at the same time, it felt like there could be more, like Teddy should be more full. And Howard just kept pushing forward.

As soon as Howard was completely buried in him, Teddy knew he didn't need to have the bike running. The two of them were shaking and vibrating quite enough without the help of the engine. He pushed up on the tips of his toes, trying to relieve the pressure in his lower back, but it didn't help. The only thing that could help was if Howard slid out of Teddy's channel, but he didn't seem like he was in any hurry to do that. His cock twitched against Teddy's walls, and each time it did, Teddy shuddered. His balls ached. His prick throbbed. He thought he might explode with every thump of his heart.

The bike glistened beneath him. The leather had never felt so smooth, so good, as it did when Teddy's crown scraped across it, smearing the precum. He had never seen chrome so bright, never seen lines so perfect. Howard moved liked an extension of the bike, like he and the motorcycle were part of the same being. He moved his hips with perfectly timed thrusts, his fingers digging into Teddy's hips, each of his moans low and hungry like the Harley's rumble.

Teddy dropped his head, looking under his extended arm to see Howard's boot on the floor. It was planted there, unmoving, solid as the motorcycle. He stared at it as Howard quickened his pace, each thrust almost hard enough to rattle Teddy's teeth. He wanted to howl each time Howard filled him. He closed his eyes, and he saw a black ribbon of road winding ahead of him, stretching into the horizon. The bike shook beneath him, vibrating from the force of each driving thrust.

His flesh burned until he thought his entire body would ignite like nothing more than a slick of oil. The thick cock in his ass would have felt amazing no matter what, but knowing that he was with Howard, on Howard's bike, made it so much better. Knowing that this would probably be his only chance to enjoy Howard's body, and the smell of his sweat, and the sound of his pleasure, made Teddy treasure each second of it. He held it all close, burning it into his memory, preparing to relive the moments over and over for the rest of his life.

Howard reached beneath Teddy's body and gripped the base of his cock, his fingers as hard as any steel cock ring. He gave Teddy a good squeeze, as if to remind him that Teddy did not get to come—did not get to have any pleasure at all—until Howard said he could. That was fine with Teddy. He was in no hurry to rush their fucking, or to lose Howard's fat cock. He was in no hurry to release the bike and get dressed again. He was in no hurry to return to the life that awaited him outside the garage, while Howard rode off at dawn.

"Fuck, boy, you're so tight. Fuck."

Teddy liked the sound of Howard's voice—like his throat was full of gravel. Every time he spoke, Teddy clamped around his cock, prompting another torrent of words. Not just words: compliments. Like Teddy was actually giving him something, actually doing something that nobody else could.

"Fuck...fuck...fuck...fuck...*fuck*."

The final word exploded out of Howard's mouth at the same moment his cock jerked deep in Teddy's body. Teddy quivered, his thighs tense, his balls tight, his breath lodged in his chest. If Howard let him come, he'd shoot all over the seat. For the second time that night, the Harley would bear the mark of his pleasure. If only Howard would loosen his fingers.

"Do you want to come again?"

"Yes, yes. Please, sir."

"All over my bike again?"

"Yes."

"Will you clean up after yourself?"

"Yes, sir. Yes. Please."

"Then come for me."

Howard released Teddy's cock, and as soon as the steel band of his fingers disappeared, Teddy burst. His cock jerked violently, and he shouted from the force of the pleasure sweeping through him. His ass clenched around Howard's cock—still mostly erect inside him—and words he couldn't control spilled from him. They were mostly nonsense, but they might have contained the core of Teddy's hunger, of his desires. They might have contained the truth.

Howard barely gave Teddy a chance to catch his breath before he swatted the fleshy part of his thigh.

"Get cleaning."

Teddy turned around, maneuvering as gracefully as he could while his limbs felt like lead weights. He lapped at the leather seat, his spunk now tasting familiar against his tongue. Howard stepped back and tucked his cock in his jeans, watching as Teddy finished his task.

"You're pretty good in the garage, aren't you?" Howard asked when Teddy finished. Teddy straightened and wiped his mouth with the back of his hand.

"Yeah. I do most of the work around here."

"Is that why you stick around?"

Teddy lifted his shoulder in a half shrug.

"My old man needs my help."

"He might, but he sure doesn't act like he deserves it. Or appreciates it."

"I...well..."

Howard shook his head.

"It's okay. This isn't a trick. You want to leave?"

"Yeah, I thought about it. But it's not like Dad pays me to do shit around here. I wouldn't get very far."

"No, you want to leave with me?"

Teddy stared at him.

"Are you serious?"

"Yeah. I think you'd be good to have around. You gotta keep the bike tuned up and cleaned."

"I'd love to do that."

Howard smiled.

"Yeah, I thought you probably would. I'm leaving at six tomorrow."

"I'll be ready."

"What are you going to tell your old man?"

Teddy pulled on his shorts, not surprised by the fact that he was still semierect. "I don't know. Nothing, I guess. I can leave him a note."

"As long as he's not going to come after me."

"I'm over eighteen and he doesn't own me, so I guess I'll go wherever I want."

His smile widened.

"Go get your shit together, kid. I'll come back up to the house in a bit."

Teddy didn't need to be told twice. The smells of leather and exhaust and cum and sweat followed him to his room, and then beckoned him beyond that. To a world waiting to be explored. To a freedom he had never tasted before.

# TULSA

## Dusty Taylor

The ride is incredible. There's a sweet spot vibration at 6500 rpm that gets right inside my recently plowed ass. It comes up through the engine and revives the bite of Rico's massive tool. I clamp my knees on the gas tank and hold tight, savoring the sensation as long as I can. The hot desert wind dries my sweat. I could go on like this forever, and the Mojave Desert seems big enough. Ride all day and fuck all night. Is that all these guys do? Rico's bankroll is as big as his cock, so he must do something for a living. And the man in the blue leather jacket? I have to admit, if not for him, I wouldn't be out here.

It was the blue leather jacket that caught my eye in the first place. *Blue* for god's sake, and the guy looked great in it. Amid the crowd of potbellies and greasy leather, his tight jeans and slim build stood out. What was he doing at a hard-core biker bar? I mean, I sure as hell didn't belong there either, but then I was *looking* for trouble. What was he looking for? He pulled up to the curb just like he belonged, but he wasn't even riding a Harley. It was a vintage cafe racer with skinny tires and low handlebars, dwarfed by the big American iron—glossy black with gold trim on the tank, just a hint of chrome, and an interesting exhaust note. I'd never heard another bike like it.

I had told myself that I would go in if someone caught my eye. Just six hours before I had been unceremoniously fired, and so I walked to the biker bar in search of distraction. The guy in the blue jacket took off his helmet and instantly drove the image of my former boss from my mind. He had a crisp haircut and a natural smile. I followed him in.

The bar seemed quiet compared to the rendezvous out front. I left a single bar stool between us when I sat down.

"Cuba Libre," he told the bartender.

"Stoli," I said. I was about to say something when his eyes met mine in the mirror. He smiled and I lost my nerve. Across the empty bar stool I felt a charge. I would let him make the first move.

A burly hand on my shoulder spun me the other way.

"Hey, didn't I see you at Frank Bonner's party last year? You remember, we all got fucked up and jumped off the balcony into the goddamn pool?" The smile was friendly and seemed genuine. "It's me, Rico."

The blue jacket regarded us openly in the mirror. Did I detect jealousy?

"Sorry, but you've got the wrong man." I tried to sound casual. "Sounds like I missed a hell of a party though."

He blinked.

"For real? Shit, I could have sworn that was you." He released my shoulder and started to turn away, then stopped. "Hey, let me buy you one."

And that's how I met Rico. He snagged me right off the bar stool, fresh meat in a market. I had never really been into bears

before, but I liked his overpowering masculinity and savored
the little victory of winning his attention in full view of the blue
jacket. There was no attitude, just easy conversation. He kept
putting his hand on the back of my neck. I admired his self-
confidence. That's what made me say yes when he asked me to
go for a ride. Blue Jacket turned to watch us leave.

Victorville was hell and gone from any place I'd ever been, but I
didn't care. The ride out was wild. Rico had a half-shell helmet
in his saddlebag that fit me pretty well, and I liked the way it left
my face in the wind. I cuddled up behind him and gave myself
over to the night. After all, short of signing up for unemploy-
ment, I had no plans for the morning. Rico was strong and
warm. That was good enough for me. We rode the midnight
freeways out of town and made his motel room at 1:56. That
should have been my first red flag.

The second should have been the gun on the nightstand, but
it's amazing how a dick up your ass can affect your judgment.
Rico turned out to be one horny bastard. Built like an artillery
shell, he was massive, with great definition of muscle, and furred
like a mammoth. I was not disappointed.

We broke the ice in the shower. Rico's pelt ran from his neck
to his crotch, his fat hose disappearing into a thick wiry bush. As
he soaped, it swung back and forth, bobbling against my hip. I
was hard in a matter of seconds. He smiled like a little kid.

"That's what I wanted to see," he said, taking my cock in his
rough hand. I didn't say anything, just leaned against him and
let him stroke me. He reached a beefy arm around my shoulders
and steadied me while he worked my cock in a soapy lather.

When I went to work on his dick it was different. Rico was
bigger than I was, and his cock hung fatter and longer. It took
him a while to get hard, but once up, he was impressive. His

enormous bone stood tall before me, as though it would crowd us both out of the shower. I couldn't wait to get my ass around it. He obliged beautifully.

Rico pinned me against his mattress and went to work. His hands were everywhere: on my ass, my chest, my cock, my face and in my hair. Never before had I been fucked by someone so eager to do all the work. He slipped down and sucked my dick into his mouth. Working just the head at first, he inhaled me like a four-horsepower pump. His rough hand stroking my shaft felt so good beside the softness of his mouth. I was no stranger to blow jobs, but this was amazing. He picked up speed, then slowed down, teasing me all the way. When he started to work his way down my shaft I had to hold back to keep from coming. I didn't want it to end. He had me so hard my cock hurt, like it was about to burst, and the pain was exquisite. Finally I could hold out no more. I felt my balls wind up for the pitch and I let go. Rico sensed it and doubled his efforts. In a heartbeat I was coming like a fourteen-year-old. I arched my back and hit him with a geyser blast, then several short bursts. I fell back limp and sweating. When Rico came up for air, his smile was gone. I knew he was ready for serious business.

Rico kneeled between my legs and pulled me close. Palming my ass, he rubbed his cock between my cheeks, and I saw the big head, now swollen dark purple, peeking up from behind my balls. He was ready to fuck and so was I. I still can't believe there's a rubber made big enough for Rico's fat choad, but he had one. He carefully slipped it on and lubed up. I raised my ass up in invitation and took a deep breath. At first he went slowly, working the head into my pucker. I relaxed and let him push in a few inches. He worked it around for a while, waiting for me to let him in. I bore down and felt him slip smoothly into me as my ass opened wide. In one long stroke he was in, and I was delirious. Still, Rico did all the work. He held me under my ass, effortlessly supporting my weight. He pounded steadily and forcefully, but not roughly. I felt every vein and ripple in his rod as it slid through my ass, and I loved it. I had never before been so thoroughly drilled. I closed my eyes and went along for the ride, with Rico's powerful engine throbbing between my legs.

I caught sight of the gun when I opened my eyes. It was a small automatic in a well-worn holster, the kind that fits inside your belt. I was a little surprised, but not frightened. As Rico fucked me I eyed the big hole in the barrel. I imagined the gun firing as Rico came, and the thought thrilled me. Then I thought of the gun coming, pumping a load of jizm onto the sheets while Rico's cock fired a bullet into my ass. The image was so electric that I felt my balls signal another go. Rico pumped faster and faster, and my ass suddenly clenched in spasms. Rico grabbed my cock just as I blew a load onto my belly. Rico came seconds later, snorting like a bull, and I swear I heard that gun fire inside my head. With nothing more than a grunt and a sigh, he rolled off me and fell asleep. I drifted off with images of cocks, guns and motorcycles flashing through my brain.

I awoke to the sound of peeing—thunderous, massive urination. Everything about Rico seemed two sizes larger than life. It was still dark but I had slept well, if only two hours by the clock, and I felt refreshed. I rolled out of bed and stood naked beside Rico's Harley, right there in the motel room, a drip pan protecting the carpet. My smile turned to a chuckle. *These biker guys,* I thought, rubbing sleep from my eyes, *they've sure got their priorities straight.*

"Good morning, sleeping beauty," Rico said, giving me a pat on the ass. I smiled and let him kiss me. "You up for another ride?" I hesitated, looking around the room for an answer, and noticed the gun missing from the nightstand. "I mean if you want too," he added. "If not I'll hook you up with traveling money back to L.A. Thing is, you make a great traveling companion." He took out a wad of bills and peeled off two hundreds, and in that moment I trusted him completely.

"Sure," I said, "I'll tag along for a while."

The sign said "Kramer Junction," but Rico called it Four Corners. Denny's was open, and Rico ate pancakes like a steam shovel while I tried to match pace with my omelet. A motorcycle passed on the highway and the image of Blue Jacket smiling in the mirror echoed in my mind. How about that? Freshly fucked by a Brahma Bull who buys me breakfast afterward, and still this guy intruded on my thoughts. What had I let slip away?

In the cold desert morning I thought of how different a Harley sounds when you're riding it. We passed the hours meandering north at a leisurely pace, following back roads and crisscrossing 395 several times. It seemed as though he was trying to shake a tail, but I looked back several times and never saw anyone. No matter. Rico's half-shell helmet let me burrow my chin into the notch of his neck. All around us the desert burst into color. Mountains in the east shone purple. Lizards darted into the sagebrush. A roadrunner detoured to let us pass. A closer range of mountains in the west glowed reddish under the bright sky. My former chickenshit job was over a hundred miles behind me, and the wide world lay ahead. I was in heaven.

China Lake, Rico called it, but I never saw any fucking lake. Anyway, the sign said "Ridgecrest." Still, it was a city of sorts, and Rico said he had business there. He bought me a helmet and a set of leathers in a shop downtown. Rico's wad had to be hundreds all the way down.

"I'll pick you up in about an hour and a half," he said. "Stick to Ridgecrest Boulevard and I'll find you."

The midday sun burned hot. I unzipped my new jacket and sauntered along the empty road. Where the hell was everyone? Suddenly alone in a desert town, decked in leather, high on the best sex I'd had in a year, I gave myself over to the moment. I was a badass, a biker bitch, hanging with a hard-core thug. I let a little swagger into my stride. If only I had a postcard, I would have mailed it to that bastard of an ex-boss and thanked him for freeing me from a comatose life in a dead-end job. Or maybe I'd go back and kick his pencilneck ass, just on principle. The fantasy made me dizzy.

I heard a motorcycle downshift behind me, but it wasn't Rico's machine. I turned around and felt myself suddenly sucked back into reality. It was him. It was the man in the blue leather jacket. Or had the heat gotten to my head?

He pulled up alongside me, letting the engine idle, and raised his visor. He was stunning to look at.

"I like the leathers," he said. "Good look for you."

It was him all right. I stood gaping, drinking him in. "Are you following me?" was all I could say.

"What makes you think I'm not following Rico?" he asked, arching his eyebrows. "Or better yet, what makes you think Rico's not following me?"

Again, I was caught short. It *had* to be a hallucination.

"You know Rico?"

He laughed a little and winked. "Well, maybe not as well as you do, but yeah. I know Rico and he knows me."

I stared at the bike and tried to comprehend what was unfolding around me. It was the same one I'd seen back in L.A., but what had appeared black at night was actually the deepest of greens. Under the intense desert sun the bike burned with color. The name TULSA, written in bright gold capitals, gleamed on the side of the tank. The slim tires and spoke wheels were of a different stripe than Rico's machine, and I had to admit I found them appealing, almost as sexy as the rider. He matched his machine perfectly, or maybe it was the other way around.

"Hey," he said, "let's get out of the sun and talk. Can I buy you a drink?"

I was starting to adjust my perception to the way things were developing. Fast—everything was happening so fast that I didn't have time to think things through. The little bike was a single seater, but I swung my leg over and grabbed his waist. My hands met on his abdomen. He mashed his balls against the tank to make room. He was trim and hard muscled, so different from Rico. The bike moved differently too, wet and fluid, slipping over asphalt like an eel. He took me down a side street, deeper into the town, to a beat-up storefront with the windows painted out.

It was a bar, and I was surprised to find it populated.

"Cuba Libre," he called, "and a Stoli," as he led me to a table in the corner. *He remembered.* I gave him a closer look. He was my age and had a gym membership; clean and smooth, evidence of a recent shave. His dark blue jeans had never seen a day's work.

"So, what's your business with Rico?" I asked, turning the chair and straddling it, reviving my newfound bravado.

Crocodile smile.

"Nice," he said. "I like that on you. Better question, what's *your* business with Rico?"

I felt myself blush and saw it register in his expression. Damn. He stole my thunder again. I just couldn't dent his charisma. Easy-going, carefree, and amused by everything—god, he was hot.

"As for who's following whom," he teased, "it looks to me

like you're following Rico. Wouldn't you say?"

I downed my vodka, looked him hard in the eyes, and delivered a line I remembered from a movie.

"I'm not following him. He's just in front, that's all."

Narrowing his eyes, Blue Jacket rested his chin in his hand. I
had never before met anyone so gay that wasn't swish.

"You do that so well," he said.

"I do what I have to do."

"Really?" he said. "And what's that?"

"I deal with events as they occur."

He took a slow breath and let it out. The electricity was out
of control.

"All right then," he said with a grin. "There's an event
about to occur in the men's room. You ready to come and deal
with it?"

The single bulb barely lit the stained tile. Three stalls, no doors,
a trough urinal and one and a half sinks defined the room. There
was a tiny window with rusted bars. Odors of pee and Lysol
battled for supremacy. He slid the bolt on the door, and we were
alone.

"You like the idea that I'm following you?"

"Maybe."

"No harm in you thinking that." He unzipped the blue
leather jacket and pulled it off. Over a black T-shirt he wore a
shoulder holster and harness. Three full clips of ammo balanced
the pistol on the other side.

I was getting used to guns. Hell, I practically got fucked by
one just a few hours past. I decided to brass it all the way.

"You're a southpaw," I pointed out. "Me too."

He said nothing but stepped in close. His hands went for
my throat, but I didn't flinch. He kissed me Hollywood style,

just like he had seen that very same movie. He tasted sweet, his tongue soft but tenacious. He explored my mouth while his hands explored my body. I noticed that he frisked me for weapons, then I forgot about it as we turned up the steam. My leathers hung open, my pants unzipped, and he ran his tongue over my chest. He twisted my nipples as he dropped to his knees and tongued my belly button. I focused on the swirl in the back of his haircut as he pulled my pants down to my knees.

He was good, but not half the cock-master that Rico was. Fair or not, I had a new standard for comparison. I gave him a minute, then pulled him to his feet. He let me turn him around and push him against the grimy tile. I held his shoulders and bit his neck.

"Go ahead," he said, "make it hurt." He unbuckled his belt. "There's a rubber in my pocket."

I yanked his designer jeans down, exposing his rosy ass and tight pink pucker—out of his pants this guy was a twink. I slipped on the rubber and lubed up with pink hand soap from the dispenser over the broken sink.

I was in with a single thrust. He cried out loud, more from pleasure than pain, and braced himself against the wall. I slammed him over and over, running to the hilt with each thrust.

"You take it rough, huh?" I said, and gripped his hair. I pulled his head back. "Where'd you learn to like it so rough?"

He said something, but it got lost in the commotion. He was enjoying it more than I was, if such a thing were possible. I gripped his triceps and leaned in hard, giving him my full length with each thrust.

"You like being a bitch, huh?" I said, and reached around to give his cock a squeeze. He was hard, and cried out, getting close to the edge. I smelled his spunk first, then felt it running over my knuckles. That sent me over the edge. I blasted him in the ass with all I had, then let him go.

"I'm going to order another round," I said, zipping myself up. "Come on out when you've got your shit together."

It took him a few minutes, but when he came out he looked just like before. I knew the rollover bitch I had discovered was gone, once again hidden deep down inside.

"Back in L.A.," I said, "you were there for Rico, right?"

"You could say that."

"And he grabbed me for what? To make you jealous?"

He smiled at that and looked distant.

"Rico has a penchant for trying to avoid the unavoidable, so I'd say he's using you as bait. But hey, for all I know he really likes you."

"I guess I like him all right."

He shrugged.

"You may find out that Rico DeTomasso is not the person you think he is, just like I'm not the person you think, not by a long shot."

Something in his voice rang true, with urgency too sincere to be counterfeit. It gave me pause.

"Rico's going to be heading north and east from here, through Trona and up the Panamint Valley to 190. That's the side door into Death Valley."

"I hear the wildflowers are in bloom."

"Take my word for it, stud, you want to be off that bike before you reach Trona."

He rode me back to the boulevard, back through the empty streets, but let me off a block short.

"This is where we part company," he said, "at least for now. Look, I'm really sorry you're mixed up in this. *Really* sorry— because I think you're terrific."

He blew me a kiss and was gone, disappearing back into the side streets.

When Rico picked me up I spilled my guts and told him everything. He wasn't surprised, or at least he didn't look it. He seemed pleased.

"What made you decide to tell me?"

I thought for a second.

"I don't exactly know, but that guy's bad news. I swear I can feel it."

"So you think I'm straight as an arrow?"

"I didn't say that. I just think you're my best bet."

"You want to split?" he offered.

"I didn't say that either."

A pause hung between us. He scanned the dusty street.

"I'm gonna put you off at the first sign for Trona. He's right, things are gonna get ugly."

Back on the road again, I watched the signs with trepidation. The morning's back-road tour was over. Now we rode fast and with purpose. Westend, Borosolvay, Argus, the mining settlements flew by in quick succession as the road started down into a valley. Railroad tracks approached in places, but I saw no train. Too soon, the end of the line came: Trona. Rico pulled over and we shared a quiet drink of water.

"Here," he said, handing me his bankroll. "If I don't get that bastard, you're going to need it to get home."

I walked the highway in a melancholy haze, the stark scenery of the desert making my sudden isolation all the more poignant. He gave me his bankroll. Was that a guarantee he would return? It felt a lot like walking money. Had I just been dumped? Kicking my heels along the edge of the highway, I weighed the possibilities. Foremost in my mind was the big question: what if Blue came out on top?

Speak of the devil. It took him maybe five minutes to catch up with me. He must have been following at a distance. He pulled up and nodded, sliding forward in the seat. I said nothing, but saddled up and grabbed hold. We took off down the road, hot on Rico's trail. Blue squeezed my clasped hands with his left and gave them a reassuring pat. My god, I was in love. These guys were so fucking alive I couldn't believe it, and I was right there with them—moment to moment, no past or future, unafraid of anything. I raised my right hand to Blue's heart. It beat strong and regular, without fear.

We rode hard, and I'd swear I could smell the big Harley's exhaust in the still air. He was close. We rounded a curve and there was Rico, less than fifty yards away and heading right toward us. He had doubled back. The two motorcycles sped toward each other and the distance closed fast. I heard the big engine race as Rico downshifted. Blue twisted the throttle and Tulsa accelerated so fast the front wheel raised up. I regripped his waist. The guns came out, Rico's in his right hand, Blue's in his left. Blue had every advantage, aiming dead on while Rico had to fire across, and his right hand still controlled the throttle. Tulsa screamed into warp speed and everything blurred.

Time stopped.

I was hit and off the bike, orbiting an asphalt planet at a distance of three feet. My throat closed up. Had Rico missed and shot me? I caught a glimpse of the bike going away from me in slow motion. It had walked right out from under my ass. I hung in silence for an eternity, then my feet yanked out from under and a concrete wall hit me square in the face. I heard my skull crack. Everything went red. I was airborne again, tumbling. The wall came back and hit me again, this time in the shoulder.

I rolled, slid sideways across its surface, then flipped over and flew, then rolled some more. I got control of my muscles and tried to curl into a ball. My skull came apart in fragments and flew out of my head. The rolling slowed, then in the space of a single heartbeat, everything stopped.

I was stuck to the wall, flat on my ass, and there was nothing but blue in front of me. I looked down and saw more blue. The sky was in the wrong place. My ears rang with a steady pitch. *Aw, fuck,* I thought, *I'm still alive.* This could drag out for hours. I hoped it was bad enough that I could bleed out quickly and be done. I lay there dying in the desert sun and waited for the vultures to come down.

And waited.

A confusion of noises crowded my broken head: engines, footsteps…a distant voice? Someone was there. Out of a red haze, a face appeared. It was familiar, but the scared expression seemed out of place. I squinted and tried to bring him into focus.

"Take it easy," he said, "you had quite a ride."

The ringing eased a little. He was giving me water. My senses began to clear. He hovered over me, bent on one knee.

"Rico?" I asked.

"Yeah, it's me kid. How you feeling?"

"I don't know."

"Why the hell did you let him pick you up? You knew what was going down."

"Don't let me suffer, okay?"

That funny smile broke across his face.

"You kidding? You just got the wind knocked out of you."

I sat up with his help. "I thought my head broke."

He laughed.

"Well, there's not much left of your helmet, but your melon looks okay."

"What happened?"

"He knocked you off, left elbow to the throat. How about that? You must have really got to him. It cost him a clear shot.

"Who was he?" I asked.

"He was a killer, kid. Not a professional, just ex-military. Ex-con, for that matter, but good. Perfected his play doing three to five in Calipatria. For now, that's about all I want to say about it. Be glad it turned out like it did. You don't want to be mixed up with a guy like that, no matter how good he kisses."

I got to my feet and leaned on Rico. He steadied me until my balance came back. My head finally began to clear. "So what now?" I asked.

Rico shrugged. "You want to keep riding?"

"Sure, I guess so."

"So where do you feel like going?"

I thought the question was rhetorical. "Where's the bike going?"

"Well," he looked across the road, "you've got your own bike now. You can go where you please."

There, propped on its kickstand, stood Tulsa, badly scratched along its left side and missing a mirror, but otherwise intact. The sleek machine seemed incomplete without its beautiful rider.

"It's a good one," Rico explained, "G-fifty Matchless of nineteen-fifty-eight ancestry, but with a custom engine—machined out of a single block of aluminum. There's nothing else like it. Nobody has any claim to it now, and I owe you. Its rightful owner was, well, let's just say a friend of mine."

Could I ride TULSA alone? Would the memory of Blue poison it for me? I wobbled across the narrow highway and ran my fingers over the bright gold capitals.

"He kind of got to me, Rico."

"I know. He got to me, too. Look, I'm not asking you to get

married, I just thought you might want to ride together for a while. And," he added, kicking the dust, "I'm sorry I used you like I did."

I gripped the handlebars and felt the familiar electric charge. Christ, the way it had accelerated! Yeah, I could ride it. I could ride it forever. And I would always remember the sexy killer who brought my butch out. *He died right there in the saddle, one wheel off the ground.*

Rico and I faced each other across the road, each of us leaning against our ride.

"So where are you going?" I asked.

"San Francisco, I think."

I looked at the arid depression opening up down the road ahead, and the mountains that rose up in the distance.

"This road lead to San Francisco?"

Rico smiled.

"Yeah, I guess it does," he said, "but by a roundabout route, you understand."

# SPEED DEMON

## Wade Johnson

My road. My law."

His name was Dimitrius.

I was just hoping for a quick fuck, so don't ask me how I ended up naked, slathered in motor oil, spending the night in a dark garage chained to a Harley-Davidson on a cold cement floor.

Couldn't resist asking, huh?

We met at a tribal gathering at an alternative lifestyle theater/performance art space. It was basically a bunch of gay guys in a big room in a circle, chanting and hollering and getting in touch with their inner *Iron John*s. I didn't know I was about to meet a *real* wild man.

We'd been locking eyes all night, my hazel eyes caught by his browns. He had long brown rock-star hair, modern primitive tats all over his arms and back, a chiseled ass and awesome boots that almost came up to his knees.

After the chanting and hollering and cathartic whatever-the-fuck was supposed to happen was over, he walked up to me.

"You were staring at me," he said.

"Yeah," was my witty comeback.

"Wanna see my bike?"

*That's not all I want to see.*

"Sure."

He led me out into the theater's parking lot. As I followed him I noticed marks on him I hadn't before, marks that weren't tattoos—marks that looked like old scrapes and burns. Was it my imagination or were some of the other guys looking at us, whispering and shaking their heads? Maybe this guy was bad news.

His motorcycle had once been beautiful, no doubt.

But now it was battle scarred and banged up, lean and mean, powerful not pretty, like its owner, I realized. This bike (and this biker) had seen a lot of action. He put his hands on the seat and closed his eyes. It was like he was communing with the machine. After what we'd been doing for the past two hours it didn't seem so far-fetched. Seeing an opportunity, I stepped behind him and pressed my body up against his.

He stiffened and spoke in a low growly voice.

"Don't start that unless you mean it."

"Oh, I mean it," I said in my sultriest whisper.

He whipped around and grabbed my face with both hands, so our noses were practically touching.

"You get me hot, you better be ready to follow through."

I didn't say anything, just stood there being held by him.

"My road, my law. If you wanna get into this with me then we do things my way. You wanna take this ride? Well, we're gonna go faster than you've ever been, man. No way out. I'll let you go in the morning but until then you're mine. Understand?"

*I'll let you go in the morning?*

Emboldened by the tribal workout I'd just had, I said: "Hit me with your best shot."

* * *

I couldn't see the bike's speedometer from where I sat, behind Dimitrius, clutching him desperately with my head down and my eyes closed, but we were going fast. Faster than I'd ever traveled on the ground before. The noise of the engine was deafening—I was yelling at the top of my voice in terror and could hardly hear myself as the world screamed by.

I was exhilarated and petrified at the same time—I knew that any miscalculation, any collision with any object big or small meant instant death for both driver and passenger. My cock, on the other hand, was having a great time. It throbbed in my shorts, smashed up against Dimitrius's butt, eager for more.

I wondered how fast we were going.

I wondered if we'd get stopped by a cop.

I wondered if I'd survive this ride.

How did I get *here*?

It all happened so fast!

I felt like I was in a trance, unable to speak, hardly able to move.

I guess we stopped, we must have, at Dimitrius's house, a little shack downtown. He got me off his bike and carried me over his shoulder into the garage. He dumped me on the floor next to a flat piece of board about six feet long and five feet wide with metal eyehooks at each corner. The Harley was rolled in next to me. He lit some candles and their flickering flames reflected off the metal and chrome of the bike. In that strange light I watched Dimitrius take off all his clothes and his boots and at his command I did the same. Then he laid me down on the board and with leather restraints secured my hands and feet to it. I made no attempt to stop him.

My prong was still rock hard, standing straight up between

my legs. With his own formidable rod stiff and ready, the biker stood above me, straddling me, with a metal can in one hand.

I watched him in the dancing candlelight, enthralled by his majesty and sensuality as he dipped his fingers into the can and brought them to his chest. Black streaks were etched on his skin as he moved his hand down his abdomen, down to his crotch. His head was thrown back and he whispered a strange chant like we all had earlier that night. I caught a glimpse of the can's label and realized it was motor oil. One oil-blackened hand gripped his big dick and jerked it. I pulled against my bondage, but not to escape, instead to stretch, to try to touch the man above me, arching my back trying to make contact with him.

Black oil dripped down onto me and as if in answer to my struggles Dimitrius began to lower himself.

His powerful leg muscles flexed as he slowly descended onto me. I arched up to meet him as his knees hit the board on either side of me. He sat down right in front of my cock, its crown hitting the place where his spine met his cheeks. He took my face in his hands and I closed my eyes. He slathered oil on my cheeks and forehead and eyelids like war paint. Then he reached his hands behind himself and grabbed my cock. My whole body flexed, stunned by the pleasure his hand brought. With one fist he stroked me, with the other himself. Then he used the oil to slick up his butthole.

Dimitrius kept chanting as he lifted himself up and then in a single movement sat down on my dick. I cried out as the biker sheathed me with his body, my cock on fire from the warmth it had been thrust into. He threw his head back and with quick pistonlike movements fucked himself with my cock. I pushed myself upward with my hips, pulling against the restraints, desperate to touch the oil-slicked body above me. It was almost as if he had forgotten me, his eyes closed, chanting to himself, like he was using me to have a solitary experience with himself.

But it felt so good I couldn't complain.

I glanced to my right where the battered old Harley stood leaning on its kickstand. The single front headlight stared at me like a blind cyclops. Or maybe not so blind—I didn't remember it facing me earlier and now it was. Was the bike watching me? Impossible?

Dimitrius flung his head forward and down. His hair hung wildly around his face, and his eyes burned into mine with an intensity that was not civilized. His eyes were not those of a sane man. With a ferocity I'll never forget he increased his fucking speed, going up and down with machinelike precision, his legs and abdomen blurring in my vision, as if going faster than possible.

Than possible for a human anyway.

The biker's whole body seemed to glow in the dark garage, then almost to become transparent—I could see through the skin and muscle and bone and see my cock as he raped himself with it. The speed of it all was wearing me out. I stared up at him without blinking, my mouth hanging open in ecstatic disbelief. It wouldn't be long now—I was being brought to climax with no participation of my own. I was being used like a disposable sex toy.

But how could I object as the greatest orgasm of my life exploded within me? I cried out again, and this time the sudden sound of the motorcycle's engine answered me, even though no one had turned on its ignition. Or was Dimitrius making those sounds?

The wild man jerked himself to ejaculation as his muscles clenched my dick, which was still spurting deep inside him. Dimitrius aimed his tool and shot his load all over me—ropes of jizz splattering onto my chest, neck, face and hair. It may have been the shock waves of ecstasy rolling over me, but the biker's cum didn't look white.

It looked black.

Motor-oil black. And it was all over me.

The wild man suddenly stood straight up in one movement. I whimpered as my cock popped out of him with a sloppy slurp. He looked down at me, as if seeing me for the first time in hours.

"That was fuckin' hot, huh?" he asked.

"Yeah..." I gasped, "in-fucking-tense. Could you take these restraints off of me now?"

"Oh, sure," he said, kneeling down and releasing my arms and legs. Free of the eyehooks, I was about to stand up when Dimitrius put a hand on my shoulder, holding me down.

"I was going to—" I started.

"You're still mine," he said, invoking the promise I'd made before. Off a tool counter next to the Harley the biker took a big spiked dog collar with a long chain attached.

What was about to happen?

Dimitrius put the dog collar around my neck and locked it in place with a padlock. I didn't resist, I just knelt there, still in my sex-trance, hanging on every word this man said. He took the chain that was attached to the collar and began to wind it around the Harley. He chained me to his bike until I had only a few feet of slack to move.

"What am I supposed to do now?" I asked him.

"Go to sleep," he said.

"Here?"

"You know a better place for a biker's bitch to sleep than next to his biker's motorcycle?"

"Am I your bitch?" I asked.

"You are tonight," he said.

"And tomorrow?"

"That'll be up to you. Now, I'm going to bed and you should too."

He headed for the door that I guessed led to the rest of the small house. He opened the door and looked back over his shoulder at me.

"My room's right next to the garage. Don't try to get away, I'll hear you. And if you knock my bike over I will seriously fuck you up. Got it?"

"Yes, sir," seemed to be the only thing to say.

Dimitrius closed the door behind me, and I was left in the dark with the motorcycle. Seeing no alternative, I curled up on the board, using my curved arm as a pillow. I slept right next to the bike so there would be no chance of accidentally pulling on the chain and sending it crashing to the floor. Luckily it was warm in the small garage, and after a long time of lying there with my eyes open, absolutely sure the Harley was watching me, I fell asleep.

I had a strange and terrible dream that I guess was beautiful in its own way. I dreamt Dimitrius's bike spoke to me, in its own machine language that I somehow understood. I dreamt it told me to get up on my hands and knees and face away from it, doggy-style. I dreamt that the Harley backed up to me and fucked me with its tailpipe—the red-hot metal burning inside me but leaving me unharmed. When it was done with me we both went to sleep.

Just before I drifted away again I remembered something the wild man had said when we first hooked up. *I'll let you go in the morning.* My last thought before sleep took me was to wonder if I would actually want him to.

# AS IT FLIES

Jeff Mann

I see him before he sees me. I sit in this busy truck-stop Dairy Queen sipping coffee in April twilight, and through the window I watch him park his bike, a black-and-silver Harley that's seen better days. As soon as he pulls off his helmet and I get my first good look at his face, all doubts disappear and I've made up my mind. Despite the risks, I'm going to do exactly as I've planned.

By the time he enters the place and notices me in my corner booth, he's unzipping his black leather jacket. The kid's a stranger, because we've never really met, but he's also a friend I know a lot about, thanks to several months of cyberspace chat, someone I'm already infatuated with. He's twenty-five, fifteen years younger than me. He's been single for over a year, after his stuck-up vanilla boyfriend dumped him and headed off to law school. He graduated from college three years ago, with a music/ philosophy double degree. His well-off parents disowned him when he came out. He wants to see America, write songs, record a CD. His bike's name is Hermes, because it makes him feel as if his heels have wings. He's been a guitar player in a metal band, a gymnast, a lifeguard. Lately, he's scraping by as a short-order cook in a college-town diner. And, most relevant to this rendez-vous, he likes older men; he's a bottom looking for summer fun, erotic experimentation with someone he can trust.

I wave. He smiles, a perfect flash of white framed by full lips and a closely trimmed black beard, and strides over. Even those few steps—long legs in jeans and biker boots—emphasize how wiry and agile he is. He moves like a dancer.

I stand, offering my hand. "Pat?"

"Yeah," he says, giving me a firm shake with one hand and placing his helmet on the table with the other. "And you must be Jesse. Great to finally meet."

"You bet," I say. He's infinitely hotter in person, downright dazzling, far surpassing the modest photos he'd attached to his messages. You'd think that months of flirting with him on a leather website and via email would have prepared me for this hunger I'm already feeling, but no. His eyes are so dark they might be black, with thick, long lashes and heavy black eyebrows. His hair's wavy, dark background for gleaming silver hoops, two per ear. Inside the shadows of the unzipped jacket I can make out very pale skin, apparently hairless, above the curved edge of a black tank top. He reminds me of the black tulips and baby's breath blooming in the holler back home.

"Damn, dude," he says in an awed voice, as our hands part and we slip into opposite sides of the booth. "You're bigger than I thought."

I grin. Taking off my Ford camouflage cap, I run my fingers through my hair, then stroke my bushy goatee. "I manage a good bit of weight-lifting in between truck runs. Does my size make you nervous?" Beneath the table, my Carhartt boot taps his biker boot. I'm already half-hard inside my jeans, knowing what's to come. Crossing my fingers behind my head, I arch my back and stretch, showing off the bunched swells of my biceps and chest against the tight gray T-shirt I wore just for such display. "I thought you said you liked big men, older men. Thought you were up for something new. After all the talks we've had on Recon Bondage, you should trust me by now."

Pat stares at me, licking his lips. "Well, I have to admit, yeah, but..." His smile's broad but his eyes are wary. "Look, uh, I gave your name and address to my roommate. Just in case..." His brow crinkles up and he drops his gaze to the tabletop. Though we're about the same height—five foot ten—it's clear to both of us how easily my bulky build could overpower his gymnastic leanness if things got out of hand.

I expected caution, and I know my way around it. "Insurance, huh? Just in case I'm psycho and you end up in a ditch?" I boot-nudge him again. He smells good, some kind of cologne: woodsy, male. "That's fine. That's smart. Relax, man. This is about fun, not fear. You wanna get some food?"

Pat looks up again, his smile broader, more genuine. "Shit, sure, dude! I'd love some hot dogs and fries! And a hot fudge sundae!"

What do these straight folks see, I wonder, as I lead Pat to the counter. Two buddies, a black-haired biker and an auburn-haired trucker just shooting the shit, ready to chow down? Several frowsy women, with puffy blonde-from-a-bottle hairdos, out with their chunky husbands and rowdy kids, give Pat's handsome face and my big chest appreciative smiles. If they only knew what would be happening later in my sleeper cabin.

By the time we make it to my truck and climb inside, it's full-on dark and we're both drenched from a sudden spring storm rolling in over the Alleghenies. Pat's never been in a big rig before, so I help him up into the passenger seat before loping around the front and hefting myself into the dark cab. Water pounds the windshield and pours down the glass. He's giggling like a little boy, shaking water out of his hair, brushing it off his leather-covered shoulders.

"Cold! Hell!" Pat shivers, zipping up his jacket and hugging himself. A chill has moved in with the rain, thoroughly dousing the day's previous balminess.

"I got several things to warm you up." I tip off my Ford cap, water dripping off its brim, and wring the rain from my thick goatee. From behind the seat, I fetch a bottle. "First of all, Gentleman Jack. Bought just for this occasion." Unscrewing it, I lift it in a toast—"Welcome to Asgard!" Taking a mouthful, I hand it over.

"Thanks, man! And I got a blunt in my jacket we can light up later." Pat downs a big gulp, then another. Lightning highlights his face for a split second—dramatic contrasts of white teeth, pale skin, dark eyes, beard, hair. "So, Asgard? Home of the Norse gods, right?"

"Yep. I was always big on Thor. Could relate to him. Drinking, feasting, fucking, butt-kicking...he and I have the same hobbies." My sodden T-shirt is suddenly freezing, so I pull it with difficulty over my head like a too-tight skin, an old life outgrown. "This here, this little pewter cross I'm wearing," I say, lifting the pendant, then letting it drop back against my bare chest, "is a Thor's hammer."

"Cool!" He hands me the bottle with a smile, raking his eyes over my shirtlessness. "Damn, man, you're so hairy, and you look so strong. I feel like a shrimp. I don't even want to know how much you bench-press."

I look down over my torso, and for a second we're both admiring the hard contours revealed by distant parking-lot lamp-

light. Years of gym-sweat, joint-pain and regular barbell struggle
have carved my pecs and the bushy gully between them.

"You like me?" I say, taking a big swig to mask anxiety,
mutual attraction being a damned rare occasion in any life.
Reaching over, I squeeze his arm. "'Cause I'm sure liking the way
you look." He's lean, yes, but muscly, too. Beneath my fingers, I
make out little biceps, hard and round as a billiard ball.

"Oh, yeah," Pat whispers, flexing beneath my hand. "You're
*awe*some. You're really, really hot. Even more than I'd hoped.
I guess I'm just a little scared." His hand grabs mine. "It's just
that...I was with Mark for four years, and we didn't play on
the side, and he wasn't...into what I'd fantasized about for so
long, and...after we broke up, I was so torn up that I wasn't
interested in sex for a few months...then I slept around with a
few girls—women have always liked me, you know, and it's easy
to flirt with them?—but it wasn't what I craved, it wasn't what
I....so this is a first for me, okay, meeting someone I've only
known online? And I do want to try some of that rough stuff
we've discussed on email, but... Could we take tonight slow,
please? I think I'm a little out of my league here."

"You bet, little friend. I ain't going to hurt you," I say, which
is true. He soon might be suffering a little discomfort, and he'll
soon be getting a hell of a lot more than he bargained for, but he
won't really be harmed. "Take off your jacket, Pat-buddy. Come
over here. I'll warm you up. There's no rush. Neither of us have
anywhere we need to be. Let's us just drink a little and relax,
listen to the rain."

Pat obeys, shucking off the leather like a pupa's lustrous husk
as the storm makes a vibraphone of the truck roof. Black tattoos
I can't make out, reduced to uneven smudges in the dim cab,
curl around Pat's sinewy arms, knotted Celtic and thorny tribal
designs he's told me about online. He scoots across the seat and

leans against me, releasing a shaky sigh. I can feel him trembling, can feel how cold his skin is. His cologne fills the cab, mingled scents of evergreen and lime. I wrap an arm around him, stroke the fine hair on his forearms. For a long time, we just sit there without words, passing the bottle back and forth, warming one another while the storm surges around us, hammering our dry little haven.

The pot's fucking fine. We pass the joint back and forth, then soothe our smoke-burnt throats with more bourbon. I'm pretty buzzed, sprawled against pillows. Pat's nestled in the crook of my arm, head on my shoulder, alternately giggly, morose, adorable, and chatty with weed and booze. We've kicked our boots off, covered up to our waists in a blanket; the rain's still drumming on the roof; I have a little night-light burning. We're both eager to fuck, I think, but it's sweet just to cuddle here and enjoy some chemical adjustment before the coupling commences. My sleeper cabin's always cozy, a bird's nest or bear den—I have several quilts and comforters in here, lots of soft pillows—but it's a hell of a lot cozier with a slender, bearded beauty like Pat in my arms.

"I still miss him, Jesse." Pat's giggles have turned to sad sighs. "We were together for four years, but, by the end, Mark didn't seem to care about me at all. I just don't get it." He coughs, snubs out the last bit of joint in a coffee cup I offer him, then rolls on his side, resting his head on my chest, and rubs my ribs with his still-moist beard. "I don't know why I can talk to you so honestly. I guess 'cause we've been going back and forth online for so long, getting to know each other. Somehow, I feel like you'd understand, considering what you'd told me about..." One hand reaches up, fools with my Thor's hammer, then fondles the curls of hair covering my chest.

My turn to sigh. I don't remember when I was last touched so gently by a man I was so avidly attracted to. Since Rob, I guess. "My soldier boy? Yep, I understand, for sure." Rob, the hot lover I used to fucking adore, till he was shipped off to Iraq, survived a lot of skirmishes, came home without an arm, found religion, turned straight. "That's been five years ago, but, shit yes, I know how you feel. I've been lonely ever since. And let me just say"—I swig the last of the bourbon—"that I've had a lotta men since he and I parted ways, but you, little man, are the hottest. And I ain't really even had you yet." I comb my fingers through his thick hair. "How you doing? Relaxed? Warm enough?"

Pat wraps his arms around my waist, tugs at the auburn fur dusting my belly. "I could be warmer, dude. Will you please…will you…will you lie on top of me? That'd be fucking awesome."

So sheepish, so young. So frigging cute. "Yep, sure," I chuckle. "But first…?" I tug at his tank top.

He gets the hint. Rising to sit cross-legged beside me, he wiggles out of the garment, then tosses it across the cabin. "Here you go," he says, smiling that brilliant smile.

"Good boy," I mutter, as thunder growls in the distance. Despite the bourbon, his long-awaited half-nakedness has me completely stiff. "Damn, you're fine." I run my calloused fingers over his chest. Pat closes his eyes, sinking into caresses he's obviously starved for. His torso's pale as a painter's canvas, soft and very smooth, other than thin rims of hair around his tiny nipples, a smoke-puff between his pecs, a dusting over his flat belly. Somehow the contrast between my bulk and his wiriness, between my hairiness and his smoothness, makes touching him all the richer.

He stretches out on the mattress. I lie on top of him, gazing into his eyes, playing with his silver earrings.

"Am I crushing you?"

"No," says Pat, wrapping his arms around me. He's so pretty that I could just lie here, poring over his face, feeling his chest against mine, but he's ready for more, I can tell by the way his hard-on is rubbing against me, how his tongue's swirling through my goatee. "Your weight feels great. Even better than I imagined. You want to kiss me, dude?"

I need no further invitation. I push my mouth against his, lick his lips, tongue his teeth. He responds in kind. We kiss, hard and deep, for a long time, pulling apart to pant and grin before diving in again, tongues butting, sliding along each other till our beards are wet with each other's spit. We roll across blankets, intertwine legs, the taste of bourbon and pot tingeing our tongues. He fumbles with my jeans, I tear at his, and soon enough we're in nothing but underwear, my cock-hard boxers bumping his dick-thick black briefs.

Our hugging and rolling grow rougher, grading into wrestle and grind. I nip his neck, the arch of his chest. He flinches and laughs, grips my shoulders, foolishly tries to hold me down. "Yeah, fight me," I gasp. He's stronger than he looks, but I have size on my side. Hooking a leg about him, I flip him onto his belly and fall heavily atop him, pinning his arms inside a firm bear hug.

Pat's giggling again, catching his breath. He tries to rise, twisting against my grasp, his butt nudging my crotch, then gives up, slumping onto the blanket. "Whoa! Damn, man, you got me!"

"You don't know how right you are," I say. "You ready for more?" I kiss the back of his neck, his shoulders' white softness, some tattooed letters there I can't make out, then grasp his wrists, gently maneuvering his arms behind his back. "You said you'd been aching to try some kink, right? We're buddies now, Pat. We've been buddies long before tonight. No one's gonna hurt you, except in ways you might enjoy. You gonna keep quiet and behave? I promise to make it worth your while. I'll give you all the wild stuff you've been refused."

Pat lies there, panting for a few suspenseful seconds. He squirms around, trying without success to free his wrists. Then he takes a deep breath and nods.

"I'm gonna cuff you now, okay?" With one hand, I grip his wrists; with the other, I fetch black circlets hidden beneath a pillow.

"Yeah," breathes Pat. "Do it, dude."

A few seconds, two metallic clicks, and everything's changed. The wild-winged biker boy's my prisoner. We lie face-to-face, on our sides. His eyes are wide, not with confusion or fright, but something else, a dark melting, a yielding and longing that make me catch my breath, that start a throb inside my throat.

I smooth his mustache with a thumb and forefinger. "I told you online that I like getting a guy helpless before I make love to him. Tonight that's you, all right? You *did* expect some of this? Hell, didn't you downright beg for it?"

"Yes," he sighs. "I want this too. I was hoping for it. I just put up a little struggle 'cause I knew it'd turn you on."

"Little tease." I laugh, slipping my boxers off. "Suck," I say, pushing his head down. Obedient, he slides along the mattress, natural grace hampered by his bonds. "Holy *hell*, man, it's so damn—" he manages to get out before I push myself between his lips. I cup his head in my hands, close my eyes, and ride his mouth, the sounds of his sucking and lapping as much a liquid comfort as the sough of storm outside. He coughs, he gags. I pull out, I stroke his head, then we begin again.

"You keep 'em in, Pat, or I'll tape 'em in and then take a belt to your ass. All right?"

My lean little biker nods, his white teeth sunk into the balled-up cloth of his own black briefs. He groans while I suck and suck and suck his little nipples till he can't take any more. He cries out—half-choked-back, cloth-stifled shouts I cherish—while I nibble his curved pecs, hard muscles straining inside the nets of rope I've woven tightly about his torso and tattooed arms. He shudders and moans—precious little "Uhhhs" and "Ohhhs"—while I deep-throat his long, thin cock, teeth-tug the black bush of his pubes, massage his balls, tickle his taint. He yelps and whimpers, writhing in his bonds, while I bite and slap the hard hills of his ass. His buttocks are the white satin of orchard blossoms, apple, peach or pear.

Pat's on his knees, face pressed into a pillow, ass in the air, thighs spread, cuffed hands quivering in the small of his back. I kneel behind him, between his legs, tugging softly on the dark thicket around his hole. The black hair reminds me of dense laurel groves that grow in mountain dells hereabouts, dells filled tonight, no doubt, by fog descending in the wake of hard rain. I run my shaggy chin up and down the cleft, bite the cheeks a few more times, then bury my face between them, lapping his little hole, giving it the veneration it deserves, stabbing and teasing the tight rose with my tongue.

Pat's on his back, calves resting on my shoulders—for a boy so smooth up top, he has very hairy legs—and I've got the tube of lube in my hand, ready to open him up with my fingers. But his brow furrows and he's shaking his head, so I pull the briefs from his mouth.

"How you doing, kid?" I say, chucking his chin.

"Hey, Jesse, look, man, these cuffs are really starting to hurt, and I don't know if I can take your cock. I haven't been fucked in a long time, and, man, you're really big. So…"

As soon as my little captive says this, I feel my own exhaustion, a combination of the booze, the weed, and today's long haul from Florida. "Sure, kid." A few minutes later, he's uncuffed, untied. I rub his wrists till he's feeling better, we both use the piss bottle, and then I spoon him beneath the blanket. The bed's pretty small for two grown men, but this just makes close cuddling required.

"I'm sorry, dude," Pat murmurs against my cradling arm. "Maybe in the morning? Do you need to come?" Nestling his butt in my lap, he reaches back to pat my flank.

"Naw, I can wait. I'm wiped anyway. Right now, though, do you still want...since you said online...?"

"Yeah, please. That'd be cool," Pat whispers. "Set me up for the night. That'd be fucking sweet. *Man*, I've been jacking off for weeks imagining this. I can't believe I've met a dude who wants what I want. Being cuffed feels fucking fan*tas*tic!"

That's all I need to hear to fulfill one mutual fantasy. I cuff Pat's hands again, this time in front of him, setting the ratchets so they won't accidentally tighten. I roll up a camo bandana, knot its middle, push the knot in Pat's mouth, and tie the ends together, not too tight, behind his head.

"Good? Comfortable?" I say, pulling him close. "You want this all night?"

"Uhhh *hukhhhhh*!" Pat nods, sighing with satisfaction. We fall asleep to the unceasing sound of rain, his back against my chest, my hands stroking his hair, my lips tracing the tattooed letters across his shoulder blades.

Pat's still curled against me when I wake at dawn. The rain's softer now but still pattering the roof. Crawling off the bed, I use the piss bottle. Pat stirs, rolling over onto his other side; the blanket slips off him onto the floor. I kneel by the bed, studying his nakedness, listening to the little whiffles of his sleep. Bruises my teeth left scatter his torso and buttocks; his biceps are marked up as well, from his struggles against the rope that bound him. His cuffed hands are tucked under his chin, as if he were praying. The green cloth is still knotted in his mouth, dark with saliva. Already I adore him. How could anyone not cherish such a beautiful boy? Not risk everything to keep him from vanishing?

I'm about to tuck the blanket back around him when his eyes open. He yawns around the gag, rubbing night from his eyes. He stretches, and we both watch his cock slowly stiffen and rise from its cloud of black hair. He jacks it with one cuffed hand and looks up at me with tacit invitation. I slide onto the bed behind him, squeezing his pecs, fisting his dick, nuzzling the back of his neck. The tattoo I couldn't make out last night is clear this morning: across his white shoulder blades, black letters edge-shaded with gray say, "KISS THE JOY AS IT FLIES."

Pat thrusts into my hand, pushes his chest against my rough fingers, grinds his ass against my crotch. I can make out what he's mumbling despite the cloth between his teeth. "Yeah. Yeah. I'm *ready*, man. I need you in me. *Please*, man. I need you *in* me."

Fucking him takes hours, patience, and lots of lube. He's very tight. I heave him up onto his knees and elbows, and for a good half-hour I feast on his ass. I kiss his bruised buttocks, beg him to relax, probe him with lubed fingers. I stretch out on the bed and he straddles me. Wincing, grunting, teeth gnashing the gag, he sits on my cock, cuffed hands resting on my chest. He's so tight that for a while we're both in pain.

Then, just about the time the sound of rain stops and birdsong begins, he's open, my cock's completely inside him, he's grinning, clamping and releasing my shaft with newly discovered skill, bouncing in my lap. I pull out, make him beg. I push him roughly onto his belly, spread his thighs wide, slide inside him.

I slip my arms under his armpits, hold him down, and give it to him hard. He's hungry now, he's hot for it, moaning into the gag, nodding, pleading for more. I bend him over the edge of the bed, pound him steadily for a long time. Growling, I grip his hips, ride him on his elbows and knees; whimpering, he rocks beneath me. Finally he's on his back, ankles crossed behind my neck, my mouth on his mouth, on his bruised chest, my hands forcing his hands above his head. His eyes are wide and dark, glistening. A few tears spill over. I lick them up and hammer him harder.

And then his eyes are full of surprise. He's shouting, his head's tossing, his hole grips me like a fist grips a spear, and he's done, shuddering and bucking while his cum spouts up and over, a huge load, covering his chest and belly. I pull out, shuck off the condom, and spurt my own sticky bliss over his beard. He lies there, panting and shaking, while I rub my cum into his face, then lap up a few mouthfuls of his juice, spreading the rest of it over my goatee.

"Let me feed you," I say, and he does. I'm dressed in yesterday's clothes, sitting on the bed's edge. He's naked on the floor at my feet, leaning back against the bed, bandana hanging loosely around his neck, legs crossed, cuffed hands in his lap, taking bites of sausage-and-egg biscuit, sips of coffee.

"That's never happened to me before," Pat says, shaking his head with disbelief before accepting another bite. "Coming without my dick being jacked. Wow, dude. A sore asshole's a small price to pay. I'm going to be wanting more of that."

"Glad you think so. I'm pretty good at finding a boy's sweet spot," I say, smirking. "So what's the tattoo about? On your shoulders?" I run a finger along the letters.

"Liner notes from a CD I listened to in college. Borrowed from William Blake. The whole thing goes, 'He who binds to himself a joy does the winged life destroy. He who kisses the joy as it flies lives in eternity's sunrise.'"

Damn, the kid could be reading my mind. "Huh. Well, maybe. Blake must have had the self-control of a saint, though. You had enough coffee?" When Pat nods, I swig what's left in the Styrofoam cup, crumple up the empty bag and wrappers.

"So, Pat," I say, pulling a roll of duct tape and some rope from a drawer beneath the bed. "I need to head out soon. Got a cross-country haul coming up. All the way out and up to British Columbia and back."

"Yeah, dude...okay." Pat looks up at me, a sad crease between his brows. Wiping a crumb from his lips, he mutters, "I was hoping we could hang out today, but if you want me to leave..."

From my pocket I pull a key ring, select the cuff key. Pat gets to his knees and lifts his hands. I free one wrist, then, before he can react, shove him onto the floor, wrenching his arms behind him. A second's struggle, a quick click, and he's cuffed again. "What the hell?" Pat says, squirming beneath me—this time his resistance's sincere, not a coy tease—but now I'm undoing the bandana around his neck, stuffing the central knot into his shocked shouts, retying it behind his head. I heave him onto his back and sit on his chest. He does his best to buck me off, but I'm too heavy for him. Quick rip of duct tape, a little more suppressing of Pat's struggle, and the strip's pressed over his lips, his beard, around the back of his neck, over and around, over and around, three tight circuits to keep him quiet. Sitting on his legs to subdue his panicked kicks, I tape his ankles together. He's still yelling as I drag his trussed form onto the bed, still yelling as I hogtie his ankles to his wrists. Forcing him onto his side, I stretch out beside him, our faces inches apart.

"Pat." I slap the side of his head, lightly, and clamp my hand over his protests. "Shut up, Pat. Listen to me. I told you before I ain't gonna hurt you. I swear. Shut up now."

His black eyes are glassy with shock, but he obeys, falling silent, breathing hard through his nose. His body's rigid with resistance against me.

"I want to keep you for a while. I ain't too good at loving the joy as it flies, got to admit. Now that I've met you, I want to hold on to you as hard and long as I can."

Pat shakes his head, murmuring what has to be "Please." His shoulders heave. I grip his hands, and his fingers fumble inside mine, a futile fight.

"We've talked about this, remember? Surely you knew this might happen. You had 'abduction scenes' listed as a fantasy on your profile page, for fuck's sake. I just want to hold on to you for a while, possess the joy, right? So, look," I say, smoothing the strip of silver-gray against his beard, running a finger along the furrow his lips shape, "if you really don't want to stay, well...just think about it, okay? I'm going to load your bike in the back of the rig, and then I'm heading up 81. It's about two hours north to the Raphine truck stop. If, by the time we get there, you decide you want loose, I'll let you loose, to bike back to your life and that dead-end diner job. If you want to stay, I'll let you call your boss to tell him you quit, call your roommate to tell him you're all right and won't be back for a while. Okay? And, yes, since I guess this is kind of a kidnapping, if you're so pissed you want to call the cops, I won't stop you."

Pat stares at me, black brows knitted together, mumbling something I can't make out. I brush his cheek; he closes his eyes and leans into my touch.

"You're safe with me, little guy. We're good together," I say, cupping his face in my hands. "Didn't you say online that you were looking for a man to own you? Didn't you say you wanted to see America? Hell, stay with me, be my boy, and I'll show you, hell, the Catskills in winter, and Iowa's cornfields, and the Great Lakes iced over, and Arizona's cactus-thick deserts, and bald eagles off the coast of British Columbia, and the redwoods, and fog rolling off the Pacific... Don't you want to see all that?"

Pat opens his eyes. He takes a deep breath, releases it, and nods.

"You're so pretty. I've never had a boy pretty as you, Pat. I'll make love to you from one end of this continent to another, as gentle or rough as you want. I'll suck you, fuck you, spank you, whatever you want. Let me keep you for a while. If it doesn't work out, if we start to make each other crazy, then you're free to leave. I'll give you the money to get home."

Suddenly it's hard to look him in the eyes, but hope crazes me, won't let me shut up and shield myself in silence. "This is how it'll be. Part of the time I'll keep you tied up back here, part of the time you can ride up front with me, see all that can be seen, help me load, unload, and haul. You'll be my captive and my comrade, in whatever proportion pleases you. Every night I'll hold you. I'll take good care of you."

Pat slumps against me. I finger a nipple, reach down for his dick and find it as hard as it was before.

"This your answer?" I chuckle.

Tape or no, I can tell he's smiling. "You can lie back here and contemplate till we get to Raphine. I'm gonna load up your bike now and start up the rig." I give his dick a squeeze. "If you choose to stay, I'll make sure your little soldier gets all the action he can stand. So you can take this hogtie for a couple of hours? You're young and limber, right? And you can breathe all right?"

Pat gives an affirmative nod. I kiss his taped mouth, then climb off the bed. With more hanks of rope, I tie his elbows together and next his knees; with a thin cord, I tie up the swollen

gloss of his cock and balls. As an afterthought, I fetch his black
and silver helmet from the floor and slip it over his head.
"Goddamn, you're pretty like this," I groan, standing back to
take the tableau in. He could be a sculpture or painting, a still
life I've helped God compose.

Tearing myself away from the sight, I rifle through his
doffed jeans for bike keys. Leaving him there in the knots of
his powerlessness, I climb into the front seat, get the big engine
warming up. Soon enough I've driven Pat's beloved bike, rusty
old Hermes, up a ramp into the truck bed and tied it down just
as I have its owner.

The truck's rumbling-ready. It's foggy this morning, a golden
dust of pollen across the windshield, the hills a fresh spring green.
I turn on the radio, low. Keith Urban, that slim-hipped Aussie,
is singing "Days Go By." I shift the stick; the truck lurches out
of Lancer Travel Plaza and forward into a future my folly prays
it might create.

My hogtied and helmeted prisoner's still hard, despite his
exhaustion. It takes me about a minute and a half to suck him
off. He lies limply as I unrope him, unlock his wrists, lift off his
helmet, cut the tape off his ankles with a pocketknife. When I
help him sit up, he groans. Side by side on the bed's edge, we
lean together in silence while I massage his metal-chafed wrists
and sore shoulders, his stiff elbows and knees.

"So what now? You want to leave? Call your roommate?
Or call the cops?" Very slowly, I peel off the long strip of tape
wound about his head; he squints and winces.

Pat reaches up, pulling the bandana from between his teeth
and over his chin, letting it drop like a pendant around his neck.
He wipes the milky ooze of post-cum off his cockhead. "Will
you hand me my cell? It's in my leather jacket. Inside pocket."

* * *

Wind pours over my face. The fog's lifted; the hills north of Raphine burn with redbud and dogwood. The colors are like stained glass illuminated from within, cream and purple fires flickering up from fissures in the earth. Everything's alive again, trees in full leaf, winter's chilly gray gone.

Pat's drowsing high in the air, slumped against the far corner of the cab. His window's half-down; breeze ruffles his hair. He's wearing nothing but jeans, feet and chest bare. The camo bandana hangs around his neck, ready for future use; his hands are cuffed before him; his ankles are tied together. He smiles sleepily at me, gives a wide yawn, and turns to look out over the hills. Then his dark eyes flutter and close.

I stroke my goatee, then lift my fingers to my nose to take in the smell of Pat's crotch, ass, cologne and cum. My mouth's still rich with his fading aftertaste. It's hard to keep my eyes on the road with him so close, his long eyelashes, his white skin splotched with bruise-black, glowing in a shaft of sunlight. When happiness is here, it's hard to focus on anything else. We'll grab lunch near New Market, turn onto 70 in Pennsylvania, catch sunset in the Midwest. There's a diner I have in mind for dinner: best black-and-blue burgers I know, plus coconut cream pie. Afterward, I'll give my boy bliss, taking him on his belly, his back, his side. I'll be joy's home for as many miles as he's willing to abide.

# ABOUT THE
# AUTHORS

**SHANE ALLISON** is the proud editor of *Hot Cops: Gay Erotic Stories, Backdraft: Hot Fireman Erotica* and the forthcoming *College Boys: Gay Erotic Stories.* His first volume of poetry, *Slut Machine,* is due out from Rebel Satori Press.

The short stories of **MICHAEL BRACKEN** have appeared in *Country Boys, Ultimate Gay Erotica 2006, Freshmen* and *Men,* as well as in *Ellery Queen Mystery Magazine, Espionage, Mike Shayne Mystery Magazine* and several other crime fiction publications.

**DALE CHASE** has been writing male erotica for over a decade, with 125 stories published in various magazines and anthologies. Her first story collection is *If the Spirit Moves You: Ghostly Gay Erotica.* A California native, Chase lives near San Francisco.

**LANDON DIXON's** writing credits include *Options, Beau, In Touch/Indulge, Men, Freshmen, [2], Mandate, Torso, Honcho,* and stories in the anthologies *Straight? Volume 2, Friction 7, Working Stiff, Sex by the Book, Nerdvana, Ultimate Gay Erotica 2005, 2007* and *2008* and *Best Gay Erotica 2009.*

**PEPPER ESPINOZA** works full time as an author and part-time as a college instructor. She has published with Amber Quill Press, Liquid Silver Books and Samhain Publishing. You can find more information about her work at pepperverse.net.

**DERRICK DELLA GIORGIA** was born in Italy and currently lives between Manhattan and Rome. His short stories have been published in *Island Boys, Cruising for Bad Boys, Pretty Boys & Roughnecks, Best Gay Love Stories 2010, Unmasked II: More Erotic Tales of Gay Superheroes, Unwrapped: Erotic Holiday Tales* and *Teammates.* Visit him at derrickdellagiorgia.com.

**T. HITMAN** is the nom-de-porn of a full-time professional writer who is routinely published in national magazines and fiction anthologies. He has also written for television and is the author of several novels. T. lives and writes in the fair state of New Hampshire.

**WADE JOHNSON** is a writer from Texas now living in Los Angeles. He was going to try to lose his Southern accent until guys told him it was sexy.

**JEFF MANN** is the author of *Edge: Travels of an Appala-chian Leather Bear*; a novella, *Devoured*; a book of poetry and memoir, *Loving Mountains, Loving Men*; and a volume of short fiction, *A History of Barbed Wire*, which won a Lambda

Literary Award. He teaches creative writing at Virginia Tech in Blacksburg, Virginia.

**WAYNE MANSFIELD,** of Perth, Western Australia, has erotic stories in *SexTime, Service with a Smile, Boys Caught in the Act* and *Wrap Me Up*. His stories also appear on the Paper Bag Press website. Find out more on his blog at myspace.com/darknessgathers.

**ROB ROSEN,** author of *Sparkle: The Queerest Book You'll Ever Love* and *Divas Las Vegas,* has contributed to more than sixty anthologies, including *Truckers, Best Gay Romance* (2007, 2008 & 2009), *Hard Hats, Backdraft: Fireman Erotica, Surfer Boys, Bears: Gay Erotic Stories, College Boys* and *Special Forces: Gay Military Erotica.* Visit him at therobrosen.com.

**SIMON SHEPPARD** is the author of *Hotter Than Hell and Other Stories; Kinkorama; In Deep* and *Sex Parties 101,* and editor of *Leathermen* and the Lammy-winning *Homosex: Sixty Years of Gay Erotica.* His work's also appeared in over 300 anthologies. He rides a Yamaha and hangs out at simonsheppard.com.

Residing on English Bay in Vancouver, Canada, **JAY STARRE** has published gay fiction in over four dozen anthologies including *Best Gay Romance 2008, Best Gay Bondage, Bears, Surfer Boys* and *Special Forces,* as well as his novel *The Erotic Tales of the Knights Templars.*

In 1996, **DUSTY TAYLOR** rode over three thousand miles of California back roads on a 1958 Matchless G50 racer. A run through the Mojave Desert became the inspiration behind "Tulsa." Today, Dusty lives and writes in San Francisco.

**XAN WEST** is a NYC BDSM/sex educator and writer whose work can be found in *Best SM Erotica Volume 2, Got A Minute?, Love at First Sting, Leathermen, Men on the Edge, Backdraft, Hurts So Good, Frenzy, Best Gay Erotica 2009, DADDIES, Pleasure Bound, SexTime* and *Cruising for Bad Boys.* Xan can be reached at Xan_West@yahoo.com.

**LOGAN ZACHARY** is a mystery author living in Minneapolis, whose stories can be found in *Hard Hats, Taken By Force, Boys Caught in the Act, Ride Me Cowboy, Best Gay Erotica 2009, Ultimate Gay Erotica 2009, Surfer Boys, SexTime, Queer Dimensions, Obsessed, College Boys, Teammates* and *Rough Trade.* Contact: LoganZachary2002@yahoo.com.

# ABOUT THE EDITOR

C hristopher Pierce is the author of the novel *Rogue: Slave* and its sequel *Rogue: Hunted* (both StarBooks Press). He coedited the *Fetish Chest Trilogy* of anthologies (Alyson Publications) with Rachel Kramer Bussel. For StarBooks Press he has edited the collections *Men on the Edge: Dangerous Erotica, Taken By Force: Erotic Stories of Abduction and Captivity* and *SexTime: Erotic Stories of Time Travel.* His short fiction has been published in thirty anthologies, including *Surfer Boys, Leathermen* (both Cleis Press) and *Ultimate Gay Erotica 2005, 2006, 2007* and *2008* (Alyson.) Visit him online at christopherpierceerotica.com.